D1526681

# *Accept This Dandelion*

## Brooke Williams

I hope you
get a few laughs
from this book!

Brooke
Willi

Published by Prism Book Group
ISBN-13: 978-1506162553
ISBN-10: 150616255X
First Edition, 2015
Published in the United States of America
Contact info: contact@prismbookgroup.com
http://www.prismbookgroup.com

# *DEDICATION*

"To anyone who's ever felt like a weed...you're not alone!"

# CHAPTER ONE

"MY FAVORITE FLOWER," Renee Lockhart said, blinking into the bright light of the camera, "is the dandelion."

The producer scoffed. She couldn't see him around the bulky black machine recording her every movement and the blinding hot lights shining into her eyes, but he was there. He shot rapid fire questions in her direction.

"You know dandelions aren't really flowers, right?" His legs shifted.

Renee swallowed. She was uncomfortable seeing only his pants and shoes. It was as if his voice came from some unknown source outside her world under the bright lights. Were they getting brighter and hotter by the minute? "I...I know," she stuttered as the sweat gathered at the back of her neck. What had she gotten into? She never should have allowed herself to be put into this position in the first place. "But they certainly look more like a flower than a weed," she continued, picking up speed and gaining confidence. Who was he to mock her answers? "And I enjoy the way they turn to white puff and spread themselves in the wind."

"White puff?" He snorted as someone else off camera coughed. "I think we're done here."

Renee's face grew warmer. She was already flushed from the heat of the lights and the pressure of the situation, but now she had to be beet red. The producer's legs turned and walked away from the set as another pair entered her line of sight. As the assistant's face brightened outside of the shadows, Renee realized what was happening. She was being dismissed. In her fury and embarrassment, she began to pull at the wires connecting her to the microphone. It had taken the staff quite a bit of time to figure out where to place the small bud so her dress would hide it, but it would still pick up her voice. Now, Renee didn't care how much effort had gone into its placement. She wanted it off. She needed freedom.

Renee shook the wire until it disconnected from the battery pack situated behind her. She pulled the microphone up and out in front of her and threw it onto the chair she had been occupying, only wishing it were heavier so she could make more noise.

What a waste of time. She should have known better than to ever agree to such nonsense. A dating show? It wasn't like her. Her co-workers knew that. And yet they signed her up for it anyway, just because they wanted her to find someone. And she, even after her doubts and misgivings, had gone ahead with the process. What harm could it do? But now, she had her answer. Renee was mortified. A man with no torso dismissed her…a coward with only legs who had never even shown his face.

THE PRODUCER RAN his hand over his semi-bald scalp as he made his way across the cold, open studio and into the control booth. The equipment inside warmed it at least ten degrees. He threw his clipboard down onto an empty chair making a nice bang. The board operator jumped and spun on his heel. The other man in the room looked as relaxed as he could be. He slowly swiveled his chair in the producer's direction, but did not take his hands from behind his head or sit up from his laid-back position.

The producer frowned and directed his gaze at the TV screen behind the other man. Renee's pink face sat frozen on the monitor, her mouth open in mid-speech. He threw his hands into the air. "I don't know what to say."

"I want her." The seated man half-smiled.

"Excuse me?"

"Her." The man released one hand and threw his thumb over his shoulder toward the monitor. "She's the one."

The producer's jaw dropped slightly. This was Ben McConnell's type? He preferred bumbling, fresh-faced girls with little life experience over all of the others they brought in and paraded before him?

"Are you...are you serious?" The producer was certain Ben was joking.

"As a heart attack." Ben swiveled the chair back around to view the frozen TV screen more closely. "Oh, and change the name of the show. We're going to call it *Accept this Dandelion*."

## CHAPTER TWO

RENEE WAS ON a mission to exit the TV studio as quickly as possible. She was sweating in places she didn't even know she had sweat glands. The lights made her hot, but the dismissal from the producer steamed her.

"Miss Lockhart," a distant voice called. Renee had half a mind to keep walking and never look back. But with her luck, she probably forgot her keys and was being chased down by a well-meaning intern. She slowed her pace, allowing the person calling to catch up.

"Miss Lockhart." A firm hand grabbed her elbow.

Renee realized too late that she recognized the voice. It was attached to the producer's legs. Looking at him directly, she was no longer intimidated. Had he sought her out to ridicule her some more?

She wrenched away from him, determined to continue her path to the parking lot.

"You didn't give me a chance to explain what happens next," the producer pleaded.

Renee had been dismissed. Rudely. What did he want from her?

"The taping will begin in one week. I know it's short notice, but we're a local station, and we don't have time to waste. You'll find all of the information you need here on this sheet." The producer thrust a bright yellow form into her hand with typed details on front and back. "If you have any questions, call the number listed there."

He turned to leave. Renee was confused. "Wait." She stared at the paper she clutched. "Does this mean you want me on your show?"

The producer shrugged. "You're on the show."

Disbelief flooded Renee as she watched him walk back down the long hall she had just run. He hadn't indicated he wanted her to be a part of the show, but she was going to be on it nonetheless. As Renee reviewed her audition, an idea formed. Every dating program like this had characters, right? There were beauties, bad girls, and even fools. There were girls everyone loved to hate. And there were always girls that gave the audience a good laugh.

Renee was cast as the fool. But that was okay for the moment. She was on the show. She didn't have to play the part intended for her. She could still raise her public profile, and, with any luck, win the job at the radio station. Once she was in the morning time slot, she would be able to enjoy her career. If she had to use a silly little dating game program to get where she wanted to go, so be it.

When Renee reached her car, the information sheet was still in her shaking hands. She had to do this. Somehow, though she hadn't signed up for the show on her own, she was going to be on it. She didn't know what might come of it, but she hoped it would help her.

Renee smiled. This would be an adventure for sure. And it all started in one week. There were a lot of preparations to orchestrate. But first, she needed to get back to work and talk to Janice. Janice was the one who signed her up for the show. And she would need to inform her boss of the time off required. She wondered how he would react.

Renee allowed herself to daydream all the way back to the office. Maybe she'd be offered the job immediately once everyone heard she was going to be on TV. Janice would probably jump up and down, yelling and screaming, which was normal for her on any given day, even when there wasn't big news.

Renee decided to visit Janice first. She was responsible for setting things in motion so she deserved to receive the details from Renee before it was announced to the rest of the city.

"Where have you been, girl?" Janice said as Renee leaned against her office door. "It's been crazy around here, let me tell you. Can you believe the sales staff had the nerve to dump their work on me again? That's twice this week. I'm not paid enough to do my own projects, much less theirs—" Janice rambled without taking a breath. She finally looked up.

"Oh right, you had the audition today." She stood up from her computer and moved around her desk, waving her hands in the air. "How did it go? Did they love you? Did you meet the man yet? Is he gorgeous?"

Renee smiled and gave Janice a coy glance.

"Well come on, girl, spill," Janice continued without giving Renee a chance to say a word. "This could be your big break, it really could. The show could work wonders for your career, not to mention…there's a man involved. Do you know who it is? Do you think you'll like him? What did they ask you? Come on already."

When Janice calmed down enough to let Renee speak, she took a seat in the chair next to Janice's overflowing desk. "The audition didn't go well." Renee frowned. "I may be able to talk to thousands every day on the radio, but when I was in a room with TV cameras...I don't know...I couldn't say anything right."

Janice sat on the edge of her desk, visibly coming down from her high-octane attitude. "Oh, sweetheart, it's okay. TV's not for everyone." She reached out and patted Renee's knee above the run in her pantyhose.

"You're certainly right." Renee kept up the charade. "I mean, look at me." She ran a hand through the mess her hair had become.

Janice sighed with a guilty look on her face.

Before Janice could voice her lament, Renee jumped in again. "It's a wonder they want me at all." She tried to hide her smile behind her hand.

"Aw, Renee," Janice sympathized. "Wait, what? Did you say...?"

Renee nodded. "I made it. I'm on the show. I don't know how, but I'm on."

Janice, much as Renee suspected, immediately jumped off the desk, arms extended and mouth open wide. "Yes! I knew you could do it. I knew a pretty young thing like you would be what they wanted. I told you, I did."

Janice rushed past her, arms still extended and waving back and forth. "She's in! She's in!" she cried as she raced up and down the hall, knocking on a few closed doors. Renee quietly returned to her cubicle down the hall.

*Well, that takes care of informing the staff.* She should have known once she told Janice, she wouldn't have to tell anyone else.

"Renee, I heard the good news."

Renee turned to find her manager standing behind her.

"You and the rest of the city." Renee glanced into the hall where Janice was doing another lap in case someone missed her first pronouncement.

"I presume you'll need a little time off?" he asked.

Renee nodded. "I haven't studied the full schedule yet, but I'll shoot you a copy of when I'll be out as soon as I get a chance."

"Good work." He smiled, a rarity given his serious nature. "You've been proactive about getting the station's name out in the public."

Renee's boss turned on his heel and left the office, nearly interrupting Janice's final lap.

Renee allowed Janice to spread the word as her mind ran a mile a minute with everything she needed to do. Her boss actually smiled and congratulated her. He wasn't even balking at the time off she would need. And why would he? It was free advertising for the station. Renee threw herself into her chair. She needed to concentrate and dig in. Instead, her face stretched into a smile so large so could hardly contain it. The show wasn't a part of her plan. In fact, she'd been reluctant about it. But now?

Bring it on.


THE AUDITIONS HAD been long and grueling. If you describe watching a bunch of beautiful women preen and primp for the camera hard work. Ben might not find love, but he was certain of one thing...he would have a lot of fun trying.

The station hadn't yet announced he was the bachelor in question. If they had, the number of women coming in to audition might have easily doubled. Possibly even tripled. He was well known in the city, after all. He had a reputation as the black sheep of the McConnell family. The one who shrugged off their business to start a dynasty of his own. And his success only heightened the interest of those in the community.

The city held Ben in high regards, but his family seemed to look down on him. Ever since he threw away all of his training in their business and began one of his own, his father had been distant and disappointed. In a way, Ben understood. His father taught him everything he knew about running the business, and he wanted Ben to emulate his successes. Instead, Ben created successes of his own. He knew that wasn't the only reason his father was disappointed. Along with business lessons, his father taught him how to have a successful family life, and Ben had failed miserably on that front. But the show could change all of that. He might be able to develop a new reputation in the community and restore some of the respect he lacked from his father. He might even be able to begin that family life that his father wanted him to have. Time would tell.

It didn't hurt that he was young, good looking, and charming as well. Just ask him. He may not be humble, but ladies loved him that way. And he had a different one on his arm every weekend. The problem with that was he couldn't keep the same one around. Not because the women wouldn't have stayed, but more because Ben didn't let them. Finding new dates was easy, but he wanted someone to share his life with, just like anyone else. And he was getting to the age where dating was becoming a bore. He wanted to settle down and start a family with one special woman.

He wasn't sure the show would help him do that. It was filled with several women that were his type, but those women were usually only good for an event or two. Luckily, a few of the women in the mix interested him. One of them might even make it to the end and beyond.

If Ben didn't find love, he was certainly going to enjoy the attention. He had a reputation with the ladies, but it wasn't often he had a dozen of them fawning over him at once. And that's exactly what they would do when they found out he was the local bachelor in question.

Fawn away, ladies, Ben thought. *Do your best.* He flipped open the folder of pictures he had been given of the bachelorettes to study their names and faces. It would help him remember them on the first night. Clara. Tracy. Eva. He continued on. Renee.

Ben stopped. Renee's picture was different from the rest. Something about the look in her eyes gave her a more genuine appearance. She wasn't a stunning beauty like most of the women. She was cuter. And she didn't have all the right answers in her audition, but he looked forward to finding out more about her.

# CHAPTER THREE

THE MORNING SHOW host invited Renee to be a guest later in the week. It was the beginning of her climb to fame.

She arrived at work hours earlier than usual, prepared for the onslaught of questions. Her co-worker greeted her with a quick smile.

"Ready?" Chuck winked.

Renee nodded. She didn't need to be nervous. She was on the radio every day. Just not usually as the subject.

Chuck let a song fade out and pressed the on buttons for their two microphones. "100.4 KGBR...Chuck and Claudia in the morning. Of course as you know, we are waiting to fill Claudia's spot, but with us today we have our very own Renee Lockhart, star of the upcoming local 'Bachelor' show. Renee, have you heard the name for the new program?"

Renee blinked. She had been concentrating so hard on the audition process that she hadn't really paid much attention to the details the media released.

"No, I guess I haven't." She adjusted her microphone to see Chuck better.

"Accept...this...Dandelion," Chuck said slowly. "What do you think that means?"

Renee sat speechless. She mentioned her favorite flower was a dandelion during the audition. Was there a connection? Impossible. She hadn't heard who the bachelor was yet and surely he hadn't seen the tape. Perhaps the producer thought her clever after all, and her answer sparked some semblance of inspiration in him.

"Hmm." Renee filled the dead space while she processed. "I guess it means deep down everyone is really just a weed."

Chuck laughed. "I've been called a lot of things, but never a weed. Okay, Renee. You didn't know the name of the show. Do I get to break the news to you as to who the bachelor is?"

Chuck knew?

"I wouldn't dream of letting it come from anyone else," Renee played along.

"Oh, goody goody." Chuck clapped loudly enough for the microphone to pick up his action. "It came out over the newswire this morning. The TV station sent a press release announcing the one and only..." Chuck paused. "Ben McConnell will be handing out the...well, dandelions, I guess."

Renee's eyes widened in surprise.

"She's speechless," Chuck said in his loud, boisterous voice. "Speechless, folks. What do you think, Renee? Is Ben McConnell the love of your life?"

Renee raised her eyebrows. She remembered newspaper articles she'd read on Ben McConnell. "Ben the Party Boy," they said. "Ben and His Babes." He may be a smart, good-looking businessman, but he certainly wasn't Renee's type. And she wasn't his typical woman of the moment either.

"Well," she stammered, "I can't say that I've ever met him so…who knows?"

"There you have it folks, Renee Lockhart, our own midday host, might be the next Mrs. McConnell. The first of many, I'm sure." Chuck laughed.

Renee forced a giggle as Chuck introduced the next song and turned their microphones off.

"Man, too bad Claudia didn't stick around long enough to witness this." Chuck took his headphones off. "You and Ben McConnell…she really would have gotten a kick out of that."

Renee wasn't sure how to respond so she smiled and excused herself from the studio. Being on TV would bring a lot of surprises. She didn't know who she thought the bachelor would be, but she certainly hadn't been expecting local womanizer, Ben McConnell.

Renee shrugged. No big deal. She wanted to fall in love, but a finding a life partner wasn't her main purpose for this adventure.

BEN SHOOK HIS head. He had a lot of work to do before the show began taping, but he couldn't seem to concentrate. This bachelor business should be a breeze. He figured the TV station was using him for ratings, and he was okay with that. They expected a good show, and he planned to give it to them. He didn't think anyone involved really expected him to fall for someone. He had them all fooled. Deep down, Ben really wanted to be in love.

Sure, he had more money than he needed, and a different woman on his arm each weekend. He enjoyed his life. He simply desired a woman to spend it with. The reason he had a different lady with him every time he turned a corner was because none of the women he met were right for him. He enjoyed playing around and testing the waters within the city, but ultimately, if he found the right girl, he would change his ways.

Ben wanted a different kind of woman. Someone who was beautiful on the outside, but also someone who didn't know her own beauty. She needed to stand up for herself, and be a person in her own right. He was tired of women who tried to cater to his wants in hopes of sticking around. Ben wasn't sure he could even describe what he wanted in a companion. But he knew that when he found her, he would recognize it. He just had to keep looking until he did.

He was excited over being on the show, though he remained nonchalant about it to anyone who asked. He had even insisted on being part of the casting process. If he had a future as the local *Bachelor*, he had to have a say in who he would date from day one. When he placed the stipulation on his appearance, the TV station hadn't even blinked. Those organizing the show wanted him, and they were willing to do anything to get him. The only compromise they asked was for none of the women to know of his involvement until the selections were in place.

Ben thought about the women he helped choose for the show. A dozen would be vying for his affection. He wondered if the city had more to offer than those who came in to audition or if the girls who showed up were good representations of the area. It didn't matter. He had hopes that he could make one of them his wife. Since he committed to going through with the dating game show, he realized it would be embarrassing to walk away without someone's hand in his.

Clara might be a possibility. She had legs a mile long and blonde hair hanging down to her waist. Besides, she indicated an interest in the outdoors, something Ben always enjoyed.

Or Tracy. Tracy had bright red, curly hair, and Ben hoped her heart would burn as brightly as her fiery locks. Something about the passion of a redhead intrigued him.

But Eva was the real beauty of the bunch. Her dark hair glistened under any light, and he thought it might even glow under the dim light of the moon. And her big doe eyes could easily draw a man in and keep him. Ben hoped she had depth to her.

Ben was also curious about Renee. He smiled as he remembered her audition. She didn't seem to be able to say anything right and in a way, it was cute. The producer hadn't wanted her on the show, but something told Ben he would never know what she would say next. And he liked that.

THE NEXT WEEK flew by as Renee busily prepared for the show. She had to get a long list of clothing items because the things requested were not attire she had readily available. As the date of the first show taping approached, Janice let her search through her own closet to help her fill the requirements.

"What's a cocktail dress?" Renee pictured the bridesmaid's gown she had in her wardrobe from her sister's wedding.

"It's something with a little glitz." Janice held up a shiny sequined ensemble.

"How do you sit in that?" she asked. It looked tight and revealing.

"That's not the point." Janice shook the garment in front of her, nearly blinding Renee in the process. Renee pushed it aside and dove back into Janice's closet. Janice was several years older than Renee, and she had a full wardrobe.

"What about this one?" Renee asked, picking out a deep blue gown shimmering under the dim light in the room.

Janice shrugged. "It's all right, I guess. I wore it to prom back in the…well…let's just say I wore it to prom."

Renee smiled and held the dress up in front of her. The color brought out her blue eyes. She imagined herself walking up to Ben and spouting off some witty line, catching his attention immediately. She didn't plan to fall in love. Though, if it happened, she had to admit, she'd be thrilled. Now that she knew Ben McConnell was the bachelor, she wasn't even half expecting any type of connection. And her ultimate goal was to promote herself and land a spot on the morning show. When she auditioned for the local *Bachelor*, she had guilt because she wouldn't be appearing on the program for the "right reasons," but knowing who the gentleman was going to be, it didn't really bother her anymore. She knew his type, and she wasn't it. Her heart wouldn't be involved at all. She could make a name for herself and let her personality shine through, hopefully enticing the city to want to hear more from her in the morning slot at the local radio station.

# CHAPTER FOUR

THE NIGHT OF the first taping arrived all too soon. Renee wasn't sure she would ever be ready, even if she had years to prepare. But she acquired the items listed on the information sheet and prepared a few things to say to Ben McConnell when she met him. She didn't want to come across a total fool.

She thought about what she might say long and hard. After all, the initial impression needed to be a lasting one if she hoped to survive the first night. She had it all worked out. On the national *Bachelor* show, girls rode up in limos and made a grand entrance to meet the man of their dreams. On the local show, Renee understood some of the glamour had to be scaled back. Tonight, Ben would hang out on the set, within the TV studio building, and wait for each introduction. The girls would meet him one by one then mingle in the adjacent set until he arrived and started the real party. Later, he would take the women on dates at other locations across the city.

First, Renee had to let the studio have their way with her hair. She wore the blue dress from Janice's closet, but the makeup crew had to get her "TV ready." She hoped to have more input later in the program...if she made it any farther. But for the first night, the crew was determined to demonstrate to her what would work for the camera.

Renee watched as they put layers of foundation on her face. She went from having a fresh look to being heavily laden with makeup. She wasn't sure she could stand up beneath its weight. She actually liked the curls they placed in her normally stick straight hair, but the amount of hairspray they used made it so hard it could serve as a legal helmet.

Renee tried not to smile or even blink for fear of cracking the makeup as she waited her turn to meet the legendary Ben McConnell. Her palms grew clammy as she began to run her lines over and over in her head.

She planned to ask Ben to close his eyes from off camera before she approached him. Once she was in front of him, she would speak and inquire if her voice sounded familiar. If he recognized her from her radio show...jackpot. But even if he didn't, she could put herself on the local map as an on-air personality. From that point on, viewers would know who she was and would associate her with radio.

Renee waited in the dark corner to the side of the set. Several other women chatted nearby, all made up more than Renee. The difference was, they looked comfortable in the finery. Renee was most certainly not.

The producer, Mike, occasionally led another stunning woman off to meet Ben. Renee looked forward to getting to know the other women. She figured they were all nice, but she was certain she was way out of their league based on the competition she spied. She would stick out like a sore thumb among them.

"Lockhart." Mike returned to the dark corner. "Renee Lockhart." He glanced up from his clipboard and caught her eye. She wiped her palms absentmindedly down her dress and wobbled forward. She wasn't used to wearing heels either, but they were listed among the requirements.

"Right this way." Mike squinted at her face as if he didn't recognize her from the auditions. "Your bachelor awaits." As they arrived to the edge of the brightly lit stage, Renee took in the living room-like setting. It appeared formal, yet cozy. A woman in a sequined dress much like the one in Janice's closet left the area. Ben turned and watched her leave and then nodded his head. It was her turn.

Renee was off set and in the dark. There was no way Ben could see her yet. When the producer gave her a nudge, she paused and reminded herself of her plan.

"Ben…close your eyes."

Ben raised his eyebrows and smiled. "I like the sound of this." He gave in to her request.

Renee took a step forward and hesitated. Everything she planned to say was at the tip of her tongue. She hadn't forgotten the lines she carefully formed over the past few days. But suddenly, they seemed hollow and empty. She made this show all about her, and it wasn't right.

The show wasn't about her or her career at all. It was about this man…standing in front of her in the living room set…his eyes closed in anticipation.

Renee approached Ben faster than the other women. He wasn't watching anyway. Once in front of him, she allowed herself a moment to study him. He was handsome up close. His hair so dark it was nearly black and skin so tan you wouldn't have guessed he was from the Midwest. She couldn't see his eyes, and she was glad.

If he opened those piercing brown eyes she had seen in the papers, she would surely lose her nerve.

Instead, she reached out and grabbed the colorful handkerchief sticking out of the breast pocket of his suit jacket. He must have sensed the slight tug because the lines around his eyes creased.

Renee made use of the handkerchief, wiping it firmly across her lips. "You've heard a lot of things from a lot of women in your life." She wiped her eyes between words. "You've listened to plenty even today." Renee paused and folded the cloth in a different way to have clean space with which to work. "What you are going to hear from me," she continued as she spit into the handkerchief, "is the truth. Nothing but the truth."

At the sound of the spitting, Ben opened his eyes without Renee's permission. He looked from her to his handkerchief and back at her. She wiped the spit-laden fabric across her cheek, removing more of the makeup.

"This," Renee said, circling her face. "This isn't me. I want to make sure you understand what you see is what you get." She wiped her other cheek again. "The truth." She folded the cloth and stuffed it into his breast pocket.

Ben opened his mouth as Renee brushed past him and walked into the dark on the other side of the set.

# CHAPTER FIVE

BEN RAN HIS hand through his dark hair, feeling the gel the production crew had placed before the taping began. It was crunchy and not the way he liked it. He was halfway through meeting the twelve women who would participate in the dating game show, and he was perplexed.

He remembered Renee Lockhart from her audition, and the several times he studied her picture since. She was a fresh-faced woman who puzzled him, though he didn't know much about her yet. When he heard her voice from across the studio stage, he was excited to see her again. He was intrigued by what she might do or say when she wanted him to close his eyes. However, when she came out onto the studio floor and stood before him, she wiped off all her makeup right in front of him. What kind of woman did that? On TV, no less.

Ben didn't know what to think, but knew he would have a hard time concentrating on the next six bachelorettes when all he wanted to do was move on to the next stage where he could talk to the few women he already met...specifically Renee. He had a burning desire to find out what made her tick. If nothing else resulted from this little program, he would figure her out.

RENEE CROSSED AND uncrossed her legs. The dress she picked was certainly more comfortable than the one Janice recommended she wear, but it wasn't something she enjoyed lounging around in. She waited on the second set with half a dozen others as additional contestants began trickling in after the short taping break ended. Renee felt a little silly and definitely out of her league. Being the only one without makeup made her feel naked. In radio, she often spoke her mind. But no one recorded radio broadcasts. On TV, anything she spoke could be played over and over again. She needed to be careful.

And though she wondered what kind of impression she made on Ben and how the viewers would see her, Renee also did not regret her actions. She had a moment of clarity before walking out to meet Ben. She wanted to raise her public profile, yes, but she started to regret the goal. She didn't know Ben McConnell, and it wasn't right for her to judge him before they got acquainted. Perhaps he really wanted to find love. Renee was single…there was nothing wrong with giving him a chance. Who knew? Maybe she could kill two birds with one stone.

Renee would never apologize for being herself. Wearing makeup and fussy clothing and heels wasn't her. If Ben wanted her to stick around, he needed to understand that upfront. The more Renee thought about how she presented herself, the more pride she felt. She probably came off as an oddball, but maybe she would stand out. The rest of the women seemed similar with their bright white smiles, long legs, and dazzling hairstyles.

If Renee wanted to survive the first night, she needed to set herself apart from the rest and intrigue the bachelor. In order to be seen as endearing to anyone, including the listening public, she needed time. One evening would not be enough to put her name out into the public or find out if she and Ben were a match.

The muted chatter turned to high-pitched squeals. Renee quickly stood from her stiff, seated position on the couch. Had someone had seen a mouse? While she danced around on the floor, she searched near her feet and held up her skirt. The rest of the women moved to the other side of the set and surrounded bachelor Ben.

Renee stopped her dance as she realized she was alone. So much for not being the show's fool. She slowly lowered her dress, raised her chin, and planted her eyes directly on Ben. He gave her a slow, amused smile over the heads of surrounding contestants. Renee joined them and hid in the back in order to allow time for her face to return to its normal shade. She wondered if the cameras caught her little dance or if they had been too busy filming the bachelor's entrance and contestant's enthusiastic welcome.

"Ladies!" Ben waved his hand in the air. "Thank you so much for coming. I can't wait to talk to you more. Throughout this evening, I promise to give each of you a few minutes of undivided attention. The goal here is to find someone with whom I can spend the rest of my life. I hope it's one of you. Before I dispense any dandelions, I'd like to learn more about you. Be patient with me and everyone will get a turn. In the meantime, have fun and chat amongst yourselves." Ben gave them a winning smile and offered his elbow to the nearest girl. He led her off into a corner of the room where a few cameras gathered to capture the one-on-one conversation.

Renee resumed her station on the scratchy prop couch. It appeared much nicer than it felt. A couple of women sat near Renee, their conversation revolving around Ben.

"Isn't he gorgeous?" The closest woman glanced over her shoulder at the bachelor.

"And rich." The other raised her eyebrows.

"I hear he bought one of his dates a car."

"Should we put in our requests now?" The two ladies threw back their heads and laughed.

"He seems really nice," Renee chimed in. She wasn't part of the conversation yet, but she needed to do something to fill the time.

The women stopped laughing abruptly and looked at Renee. "I mean...I bet he's sweet."

The first woman blinked, and the second raised one eyebrow.

"Don't you think he's kind?" She wanted them to talk about some of his features besides his looks and wealth. She hoped the participants were searching for something deeper than material things. If not, she would really stick out.

"Nice..." The closer woman leaned back. "Yeah, I'm sure he's nice." She turned away and rolled her eyes.

Renee shifted on the itchy couch. She would learn their names in time, but she didn't need to right away. With any luck, several of them would be gone later, and Renee would still be there. She hoped the bachelor had discernment. He needed to get rid of those who might only be after his money and attractive features if he was going to find someone genuine.

Renee realized she was way ahead of herself. She was also a pot calling the kettle black. Sure, she wasn't there for his fame or fortune, but she intended to use him. Just in a different way than the others. Shame washed over her. The little she knew about Ben wasn't favorable. At least in terms of his dating history. But he still deserved to find real love. And no matter what he did to other people, he didn't deserve to be used.

"Hi," a voice broke through Renee's thoughts. "I'm Eva."

Renee slid over to make room on the couch as a stunning lady sat next to her. Renee took in the woman. She was petite in every way, and her dark hair glistened under the lights. Most captivating, though, were Eva's eyes. They sparkled with depth. Renee realized right away that Eva was not only beautiful on the outside, but she had real character.

"Renee." Renee stuck out her hand.

"Is this crazy or what?" Eva straightened her short skirt and crossed her legs.

"Definitely." Renee glanced around the room. "Have you spoken to Ben yet?"

"Just got done." Eva's smile brightened her face even further.

"How did it go?"

"Great." Eva lowered her voice. "I think we hit it off. I hope to be around to get to know him better. He seems really nice."

Renee smiled. That was what she wanted to hear from the other contestants. She nodded. "Good."

"Can I ask you something?" Eva bit her lip.

"Sure, go ahead."

"What happened to your face?" Eva asked bluntly. "I mean…it looks like you smeared your makeup off with the back of your hand."

Renee laughed softly. "You're pretty close. I actually used a handkerchief."

"A handkerchief?" Eva looked at Renee's empty hands.

Renee glanced over to the corner where Ben held court with another stunning blonde. Eva followed her gaze.

"That handkerchief?" She pointed at Ben.

Renee nodded and chuckled again. Eva's eyes widened. Eva's laugh made Renee giggle harder, and Renee had the same effect on Eva. Before long, they laughed so hard, the other contestants began to take notice. Renee didn't realize someone stood behind the couch right by her.

Eva's laughter quickly slowed as she looked above Renee's head.

"Who wants to share that joke with me?" Ben asked.

Renee spun around in mid-cackle, her mouth half open. Eva tilted her head toward Ben as if to tell Renee to go ahead.

"I guess I will." Renee stood a little too quickly. The room spun, and she swayed on her feet. Ben reached over the couch and grabbed her elbow to steady her.

"Careful. Have they been giving you gals drinks I don't know about?"

Great. He suspected she was drunk. It would certainly explain the makeup incident, the loud laughter, and the swaying.

"I have low blood pressure," Renee explained.

Ben scratched his chin, then held his long, tapered fingers out to Renee. As his fingers enveloped hers, a jolt of electricity ran up her arm.

"Sorry." Ben glanced in her direction. "The static in this studio is the worst."

Renee smiled. For a second, she wondered if the lightning reaction had been chemistry between them.

Renee allowed Ben to lead her over to the corner where the lighting dimmed to induce romance. Though the bright lights from surrounding cameras were present, a few subtle candles flickered nearby to soften the harsh studio background.

Renee sank into the chair, grateful to have something sound beneath her. She was still dizzy from standing up too fast, and she didn't want to make herself look worse than she already had.

"Renee Lockhart." Ben recited her name as he leaned forward and placed his elbows on his knees.

"Ben McConnell," Renee returned. She didn't really know what else to say.

"Are you ready to share that joke?"

Renee blinked. They'd been talking about her first encounter with Ben. "Oh, that was nothing." Renee's cheeks grew warm, and her neck started to sweat.

Ben nodded, allowing her the grace to get out of that particular conversation track. "Okay, tell me about you."

"Well, I work in radio." It was best to get her job in the forefront as soon as possible. Though she was having some issues with guilt, she came on the show to make a name for herself. She would keep an open mind, but she still needed the publicity. "I'm on the midday show over at KGBR."

"Renee Lockhart." Ben searched her face. "Yeah, I think I've heard you. You do requests and stuff?"

Renee nodded. "I also do a lot of behind the scenes things like make commercials, write promos, help out at concerts, that sort of thing."

"Make up a commercial about me." Ben scooted his chair closer.

Renee frowned. "Huh?" She was suddenly very aware of the camera before her, capturing her every motion.

"What would you say in an ad for me as the bachelor?"

Renee froze. He was serious. He wanted her to come up with something on the spot to advertise a date with him. She could write, and she knew it. But she usually did her writing in a small office alone with no one looking over her shoulder, much less into her eyes.

"Um…" Renee clasped her hands in her lap and fidgeted with her thumbnail.

"Come on, I won't be offended. Give it a try."

Renee took a deep breath. She always liked to start and end her ads with the company name. "Ben McConnell," she said with a dramatic pause, "man of mystery, bachelor of the city." Renee stopped again, and gazed at Ben. For a moment, she wasn't sure she would be able to go on. The look in his eyes captivated her, and she found herself speechless…very rare for someone like her. It wasn't so much that his eyes were piercing and such a beautiful color of brown, but more their amusement and depth. Renee suddenly realized how careful she needed to be. This man could easily draw her in and break her heart.

She tore her eyes away from Ben and placed them on the camera behind them. "With dark hair and shimmering skin, gleaming from a touch of sun, and a laugh that would light up a room, Ben McConnell is the date of any girl's lifetime."

Now she was on a roll. Renee glanced back at Ben long enough to see he was enjoying her recital. She had his attention, and in order to keep it, the rest of her impromptu commercial needed to be memorable.

Renee leaned way over in her chair, throwing her arm up beside her for dramatic effect. She had the perfect line to close her short ad, but instead of delivering it, she flung one of the flickering candles to the floor with a loud crash. "Fire!" she screamed as she realized the flame had not extinguished, but rather transferred itself to the hem of her dress.

Before Renee could stop, drop, and roll, Ben leapt from his chair and threw himself across the small space separating them. The pressure of his body against her leg put out the fire instantly, but it also toppled her chair over, leaving them in a heap on the concrete.

Renee found herself on her side with Ben's breath on her cheek. She slowly turned her head, though what she really wanted to do was push him away and run out of the studio as fast as possible.

"That was quite a commercial." Ben didn't make a move to rise. "Are you okay?"

Renee wasn't sure how the dress looked, but there was no burning sensation on her leg. There was a twinge in the pit of her stomach. She nodded. "I'm okay." She met his eyes and allowed herself a few beats to study him closely. He was handsome. And now, he was even a hero. Though he wouldn't have had to save her from burning flames had she not set herself on fire.

Ben deftly got to his feet and pulled Renee from her chair as the producer rushed over and the camera operators stood by, panning down to capture Renee's smoldering dress.

"Hey, Renee," Ben whispered into her ear, "next time there's fire between us, I'm not going to put it out."

Ben turned away as the staff brushed off his coat to ensure he was okay. The producer then turned to Renee with a glare.

"Total accident." Renee held up both hands.

Mike nodded and softened as Ben clapped a hand on his shoulder with a good-natured smile. "She was just trying to make an excuse to get my hands on her."

"Let's take a break, and get this cleaned up," Mike ordered. "You can go back to the other side of the set." He placed an arm around Ben.

"Nice talking to you, Renee." Ben winked as Mike led him away.

# CHAPTER SIX

"CAN YOU BELIEVE her?" Mike, the producer, asked Ben, running his hand over the shiny spot on his head.

Ben shrugged and looked over Mike's shoulder towards Renee and the rest of the girls. Her dress would never be the same, and Ben was pretty sure he could say a similar thing about himself. Their contact had been short, but he was most certainly intrigued. Not only by the way she talked, but also because of what he experienced when he plunged across the space separating them to put out the fire.

Ben realized he had his fair share of dates in his thirty some years of life. The media painted him as a playboy with a different woman on his arm every weekend. Part of that was accurate. He did date a lot. And the testosterone driven part of Ben enjoyed it. A man liked looking at beautiful women. But Ben's problem with ladies was that no matter how gorgeous, or sweet and charming they were, he didn't experience anything special. Hence the real reason his first dates never turned into second dates. Women always wanted to see him again. He couldn't stand starting a relationship if he wasn't drawn to that person.

Ben knew he needed to grow up. He was the mastermind behind his thriving business. His forethought and ingenuity forced the photography software company he created called ConArt to go worldwide. It spread faster than the recent social media outlets. But what Ben had in the corporate world, he lacked in his personal life. He even went so far as to think he didn't know how to love someone.

Meeting Renee changed all that. Ben now knew he could feel. He just didn't know what to do about it.

Ben saw Mike's hand wave in front of his face. His tore his gaze from Renee, who was limping to the couch, and focused on the hand in front of him.

"You like her." Mike's mouth remained half open as he stared. "You like...*her?*"

Ben shrugged. "I haven't talked to them all yet." Perhaps someone else in the group would make him tingle like Renee had.

"Yes, but you specifically asked for her to be on the show. And you even changed the name based on how she answered the question about her favorite flower. This isn't some kind of set up is it?"

"What do you mean?" Ben asked. He was having trouble keeping track of the conversation with Mike when all he wanted to do was watch the contestants.

"You hadn't met her before, had you? You weren't dating before this, were you?"

Ben started to realize what Mike implied. Ben wanted to do the show, but he already had a girlfriend, so he simply had her audition for the show and placed her among the contestants. The couple would become popular in the city and would enjoy the fame the local reality program brought to their door.

Ben placed one hand on each of Mike's narrow shoulders. "I had never seen Renee Lockhart before the day of the audition." He didn't mention he *had* heard her voice before, on the radio. But even he hadn't put two and two together until she brought it up.

"Okay," Mike agreed. "Shall we continue?"

Ben nodded and surveyed the other side of the room again. He still had half a dozen women to talk to, and he chose one at a time and took them to his little corner. But it didn't matter how beautiful they were or what they said. He almost thought every woman after Renee made him experience something special, but he wondered if what he felt was residual from being near her. Since Ben never knew what it was like before, he couldn't be sure. He would continue with the show, and see where things went. It was too early in the game to decide anything. He only had to make one decision that night. Which two girls should he send home?

RENEE SAT STIFFLY on the couch for the rest of the evening, playing with the dark hole in the dress near her calf. She had no choice but to await her fate. She was embarrassed about what happened with Ben, and the other women steered clear of her. She was certain they had to be talking about her. She was a pariah. Eva stuck by her side and entertained her with bright conversation. Renee was encouraged by that. At least she would be able to relate with one other person on the show. She hoped they both survived the evening.

After every lady had time with Ben, the producer sent the crew on a break, and Ben disappeared. Mike stood before the contestants with his clipboard. "Now, each of you will talk to the camera for a confessional time. The person running the camera might ask you a few questions. Ben is in another room doing the same. We'll have the elimination ceremony next and afterwards, you can go home. This week, the program will be edited together and will air on Monday. Until that time, no one is to say anything about what happened here tonight. After the show airs, you're free to talk to friends, family, or even other media outlets. Meet back here Tuesday to resume taping." Mike tapped his clipboard. "There are three cameras posted here, here, and here." He pointed to three stationary cameras throughout the room. "When you're ready, go to a camera and do your interview. It shouldn't take long. Once everyone is done, I'll bring Ben in for the elimination."

Mike briskly walked away as silence permeated the studio. The women had been having a good time until Mike interrupted and mentioned the elimination. The twelve contestants looked at one another with questions in their eyes. Who would it be? Renee figured she had a pretty good shot at being the first to go. She made an impression on Ben. After all, she *had* lit herself on fire. But that didn't mean he wanted an accident prone woman. Renee could see her time on TV going up in flames…quite literally.

Since no one headed toward a camera, Renee decided to get her interview over with. She quickly stood, and the room swayed yet again. She needed to do something about her blood pressure. How could it not be higher after everything she'd been through?

Renee made her way to the nearest corner. "I'm ready for my interview."

The man behind the camera nodded. "Just stand where you are, and I'll adjust."

Renee waited, licking her lips and tucking a strand of hair behind her ear. Her eyes flicked from left to right as she shifted from one foot to the other. What was she supposed to do? She was an awkward mess.

"Okay," the man finally said. "Start by telling us what you thought tonight when Ben first came into the room."

"I feared there was a mouse."

"What?" The cameraman took his eye away from the lens and looked at Renee around the camera.

Renee sighed. She thought she'd been pretty clear. "When all the women squealed earlier, I was certain there was a mouse in the room. So I jumped up and started dancing around. Like this." Renee pulled her dress up to her knees and kicked her feet up as she looked down at the ground like she was searching for a rodent.

When the man behind the camera didn't answer, Renee slowly lowered her dress. "Once I noticed Ben was in the room, I felt pretty silly." Way too late Renee realized what she had just done. She hoped the cameras missed her little dance earlier. Now she was certain they had it.

"Tell us about your one-on-one time with Ben." The man's voice was light with amusement.

Renee cleared her throat. Why was this so hard? She was on the radio. But now she couldn't think of the right thing to say. "I enjoyed speaking with Ben." Renee tried to act formal. "He was interested in my career and seemed to be a really helpful person." Renee smiled. There.

"What do you mean by helpful?" the man probed.

"Well, he put the fire out when my dress ignited in flames." Oops. She just undid all the good she'd done with the last eloquent statement.

"How did I miss that?" the man muttered. "You were on fire?"

"Let's just put it this way. If Ben likes a woman who burns for him, he won't pick anyone else." Renee knew her voice was laced with the irritation she felt.

The man raised a hand above the camera. After a few beats of staring into the lens, he told Renee she was finished, and she could return to the others.

Renee stalked back into the room and slumped onto the scratchy couch. Eva awaited her.

"Did you do your interview?" Eva inquired.

Renee nodded and crossed her arms over herself to hide as much of her existence as possible.

"Me too. They didn't really have any questions. Just what I thought when he first came in, and how our time together went, that sort of thing."

Renee pursed her lips. Eva was nice, but she didn't want to commiserate.

"I just talked about how handsome I thought he was and how intelligent and charming he came across when we spoke alone."

If only Renee could have said the same thing. She wished her impressions of Ben were what was important. Instead, she brought up her own iniquities and put the focus on herself. If she hoped to make a reputation, she was doing a pretty good job. But her name might be something people enjoyed laughing over, not one they would want to listen to on the radio.

Eva grew quiet, and the two women surveyed the others strolling elegantly across the room to the various cameras for their interviews. They laughed, flipped their hair, batted their eyes, and put their hands on their hips with confidence. Before long, everyone finished, and they knew it was almost time for the evening to come to a close. When Ben entered, the producer at his side, the mood in the studio changed.

"Ladies," the producer said, "we'll resume taping in a few minutes. Ben has made his decision, and he will pass out the…dandelions in a few moments. We would like you to come line up at the back of the studio in two rows, and we'll begin as soon as everything is in order."

The contestants lined up as requested as one of the crewmembers rolled in a small tray with bright dandelions. Renee glanced at the dandelions and then at Ben. He caught her eye and gave her a wink and an amused smile. Surely that meant something? At the very least, Renee knew she entertained him. But if she stayed past the night, she wasn't sure what she could do to top catching fire. She hoped she would get a chance to find out...and to redeem her image. Leaving this early would be humiliating. Maybe, if she laid it on thick, she could talk the producer into cutting her out of the program completely to help her save face. They could start with eleven girls instead of an even dozen...

Renee played different scenarios through in her head as she took a spot in the back row with five other women. She would have to cross that bridge if...or when...she came to it. Right now, Ben got to decide, and all she could do was stand there, avoid looking for mice, beware of candles, and wait.

## CHAPTER SEVEN

BEN STOOD AT the front of the room, the confidence in his voice running down his back as he called one name after another. He had no clue how this dating show would turn out, but he knew what he wanted to do that particular night. A few women interested him, but most did not. He would get rid of two of those and keep the rest, just for the sake of the show. He didn't want to lead anyone on, especially those he already knew weren't for him.

The women he was leery of were those who said and did all the right things...simply because they knew it was what he wanted to hear. Ben suspected those contestants were after his money, his status within the city, his good looks, and the things he could bring to their lives. But he only wanted to bring one thing to a woman's life...love. His image didn't allow women to believe that, but it was true.

"Tracy," he called as the woman with bright red curly hair stepped forward.

Her face beamed under the studio lights. "Tracy, will you accept this dandelion?"

"Of course."

After she took her dandelion, Ben picked up another weed and spoke again. "Clara." Clara was one of the women he didn't think would last long, but he had to give her another chance because she was so beautiful that people might be suspicious if he let her go on the first night.

"Clara, will you accept this dandelion?"

"Will I ever."

"Eva." Ben smiled as Eva made her way to him from the back row. "Accept my dandelion, Eva," Ben said, as more of a command than a question.

"I'd love to." Eva's eyes sparkled.

Eva was one of the women Ben thought might have real potential. Not only was she adorable, but she seemed to have layers to her personality. He didn't know her well yet, but he thought she would be someone he could really talk to and enjoy. She didn't realize how beautiful she was, and Ben liked that.

Ben rattled off more names as he wondered what these women would bring to his life and if he might fall in love. He was used to being numb and uncaring, and he wasn't sure he could handle deep affection for someone.

When Ben brought himself back into the present, he realized he only had one dandelion left.


"Tracy...Clara...Eva..."

The elimination ceremony went on and on. Renee's legs wobbled like they were made of noodles. She was not going to last much longer. There was one weed on the table and three women waiting. One woman was so tall she had to be a professional basketball player, and the other had arms of steel. She obviously worked out way more than Renee did.

The bachelor paused and took a deep breath. He picked up the last dandelion and held it before him. Renee shuddered as his eyes moved over her. He was taking his sweet time inspecting each remaining option. The flower went from tall and proud to wilted and slumpy as it curled over in his hand. The rest of the weeds stayed upright as if they had a pin running through them. This one, however, had seen its best day and was well on its way out.

Ben smirked at the dandelion. "It looks like this one is about to turn into white puff."

Renee straightened her back. Hadn't she said something about the white puff of a dandelion in her interview? It was a strange coincidence.

"Yeah, this is about right," Ben muttered.

Renee took a deep breath. "Spit it out already," she mumbled as two other contestants turned and looked at her.

"This is my last selection tonight. I want to thank all of you for coming and putting yourself out there. For those of you who remain, I look forward to getting better acquainted."

Renee sighed. She really couldn't take anymore. She swayed on her feet.

"This last dandelion has to go to…" Ben paused as Renee held her breath. "The girl on fire. Renee Lockhart."

Renee blinked and exhaled. He said her name. Was that possible? She was hearing things again, right? A bony elbow press into her side.

"Go." Eva smiled. "That's you. Go."

Renee took one step forward and then another. Would her legs hold her this time? They ached, and her head spun from the long, stressful evening.

"Renee, will you accept my dandelion?"

Renee gazed deeply into Ben's eyes...and laughed. "I'm sorry." She stifled her giggle. "It's just...the way you said that...and the way that weed looks..."

Ben glanced down at the dandelion, now completely bent over in his hand as he offered it to Renee. He smiled as Renee got herself under control.

Renee forced a straight face and nodded vigorously. "Yes, Ben," she said dramatically. "I will accept your dandelion." She plucked the wilted weed from his grasp and leaned in to give him a brief hug and an air kiss as the other women had.

As Renee placed her cheek near Ben's face, he turned his head slightly to the right, and she caught the edge of his mouth with her lips. Her cheeks burned as she paused.

"I told you," he whispered into her ear so that the others couldn't hear, "the next time there's a fire between us...I'm not putting it out."

# CHAPTER EIGHT

IT WOULD BE hard to keep the news from everyone at work, especially Janice. The taping certainly hadn't gone as Renee had expected, but she was through for another week so she met her initial goal. She went about her daily business and took requests on the air. The hardest part was avoiding Janice's questions.

"What's he like? Are you in love? What did he say? What did you answer?"

Her inquisition was constant, but Renee smiled and shrugged, or nodded and ducked out of the room. She couldn't tell Janice anything or everyone would know, and she had a non-disclosure contract. The show played on the air in less than a week. They could all wait and see what happened on TV.

Since Janice failed at getting the scoop from Renee, she put her efforts into organizing a viewing party. Everyone from the station would gather at her house and view *Accept this Dandelion* when it aired Monday night. The following day, Renee would go on the morning show and talk about the experience. The only problem being, Renee first had to get through the broadcast. She knew one thing for sure…there would be plenty of laughter at her expense.

When Monday finally rolled around, Renee had nervous energy to the hilt. She couldn't do anything right all day long. She took a request for one song, but played another. She pushed the on button for the wrong microphone, making it sound like she was in a box across the room. She even let songs run out, leaving plenty of dead air for the listeners to enjoy.

The entire station buzzed the whole day, but Renee figured it was because she walked the halls, leaving her nerves here and there.

"You excited for tonight?" Janice asked. She'd finally stopped probing for details when she realized Renee wasn't going to give any.

"I'm not sure," Renee answered. She was definitely more nervous than excited. She wanted a shot at the morning show, and *Accept this Dandelion* was the center of the opportunity, but she didn't know how the editing went, and how she would come off on the show.

"Well, I'm excited." Janice whooped. "I'm making the popcorn with the old-fashioned popper. We can put real butter on it…salt that puppy up, the whole bit."

Renee laughed. Leave it to Janice to take some of the tension out of the viewing by describing her homemade popcorn-making abilities.

Janice smiled and put her hand on Renee's shoulder as the two left the station together. "Really, though, Renee," she said softly, "no matter how it goes, you are who you are."

Renee nodded. One of the things she loved about Janice was her ability to see people for who they were and to accept them as such. Janice loved everyone that came through the studio doors. She had a knack for pulling the good sides out of guests and shoving the bad away. Renee hoped a little of Janice would rub off on the entire city that night...just in case she came off as silly as she suspected.

A few hours later, Renee sat on Janice's plush pleather couch, waiting for the endless commercials to come to a close. It was the one time when she didn't mind advertisements taking up her time. She had Chuck, the morning show guy, on one side and Al, a salesman, on the other. Janice stood behind her with the large bowl of popcorn, and the others sat in chairs around the room, waiting for Renee's big debut.

When the soft, dramatic music began, the voiceover announcer spoke about the city's most eligible bachelor. Renee tensed. *Here goes nothing.*

The show began harmlessly by showcasing Ben and shots of him around the city. They made it sound like he was all alone in the world and nothing would complete his life except a woman. Renee rolled her eyes. From what she understood about Ben's dates, he wasn't lonely. Much less the hopeless bachelor they were making him out to be. But the shots of the city were nice, and the camera crew did a good job.

The voiceover announcer got to the grit of the matter. "Over the next few weeks, twelve women will compete to win Ben's heart. In the end, he can only have one, but in the meantime, they will all be dandelions in the field of love."

Renee snorted, and Chuck glanced in her direction. *Dandelions in the field of love? They may as well call them cheese on a pizza.*

The first commercial break gave Renee a chance to decompress. Her shoulders were wound tighter than ever, and she needed to relax or she would spring across the room against her will. She munched on some popcorn in an effort to appear calm and collected. She really should have viewed the show alone. Not only

[43]

would the others present be able to watch her antics on screen, but they could also see her reaction to those moments.

When the program resumed, the announcer briefly talked about each woman, showing headshots of them all. The room erupted in cheers when Renee's face appeared on the screen, and she tried to enjoy the last moment of pride she would likely have throughout the viewing.

Before long, the women walked one by one into the studio to meet Ben McConnell. Janice stood nearby making comments. An overdone blonde walked up to Ben. "She's so fake. And look at that dress." Her only remark regarding Eva was a quick one. "Cute."

The room went from active and loud to quiet when Renee's voice permeated the screen, asking Ben to close his eyes. Renee stole a glance at Janice, whose eyebrows shot into the air. When Renee walked into view, the room erupted into cheers yet again.

"Shhh," Janice commanded. "I've got to see this."

Renee approached Ben and began methodically wiping the makeup off after jerking the handkerchief from his pocket. She gave her little speech about honesty and then turned and brushed past him, leaving Ben with a look of confusion and awe.

"Oh no, you didn't." Janice slapped her hand down on Renee's shoulder.

Renee laughed. Her co-workers reacted well to her introduction. She came off as a girl who knew what she wanted...and one who was honest, upfront, and true to herself. So far, things weren't going half bad.

Renee watched as the other women met Ben, and she tried to judge his reaction to them as they paraded their one-liners...and their long legs... in front of him. She couldn't tell what he thought, but his eyes definitely sparkled when Eva first appeared. He seemed intrigued by Tracy too, but otherwise, his expression was the same every time someone new came out.

Renee wasn't one to judge. After all, she just met the man herself. She certainly couldn't know his tastes. She only hoped she could fit in enough to stick around a while longer. Though she was certain she and Ben wouldn't be a match, she needed to finish putting her name out there in order to secure the morning show job she longed for. Knowing Ben had a crop of beauties from which to choose alleviated her guilt over being there for her own personal reasons.

Renee was so lost in her thoughts that she almost tuned the broadcast out entirely. When the room erupted into a fit of laughter, she placed her focus back on the big screen TV. A very large version of herself jumped around in her fancy dress, and squealed with the skirt lifted to her knees. The other women greeted Ben in the background. So they'd caught her little faux pas after all. Renee supposed what she said on camera later made no difference since everyone witnessed her dance firsthand.

Janice grooved behind the couch, and Renee slumped father down into the seat. Being there with her co-workers had not been a good idea. She should have taken the weeks off completely to hide. And possibly never come out again.

The women met with Ben alone on screen while Renee's co-workers commented. She almost couldn't stand the agony of waiting for her turn, but at the same time, the last thing she wanted was to see the candle incident. When the next commercial aired, she knew she would be next, so she excused herself and took an extra-long time in the bathroom down the hall.

She could tell by the gasps and laughter leaking through the door that she had avoided her big TV moment. However, her problem was the restroom had no windows. She couldn't crawl out and return to her car. She had to face the crowd.

Renee took a deep breath as she washed her hands and studied her face in the mirror. She was used to radio, and she liked that world. She sat in a studio by herself all day, talking to a bunch of people who didn't talk back. She wasn't accustomed to having everyone stare at her, and it was hard to think that her experience would be cemented into TV history.

She dried her hands on the small towel. It was now or never. She slowly opened the bathroom door and walked back down the hall, knowing she had no other choice.

"Renee, Renee, Renee," her co-workers chanted. Renee turned to the TV in time to see her interview where she danced yet another jig. The chanting grew louder.

Renee could rush off in embarrassment, but she had played a part on the TV show, and she had to face it. The best thing to do was to own it. Instead of lowering her head and plopping onto the couch in shame, she simply raised a pretend skirt and began dancing.

Her co-workers laughed and clapped and settled in to see the rest of the show. The women discussed their meetings with Ben on camera, and Renee thought her eyes would roll out of her head. They all described him like eye candy and many said the meeting had gone so well they would surely be his woman at the end. Renee wasn't sure what bothered her more, the women's descriptions of Ben or their overconfidence.

When the screen cut to Ben's face, Renee sucked in another breath and leaned forward. This she wanted to hear.

"I'm really lucky to be dating all of these lovely women at once." Ben gave a cocky grin. "Any man in the city would give anything to take my place right now. I mean, I've got twelve women throwing themselves at me." He chuckled. "One even lit herself on fire. Can you believe it?"

Renee's mouth gaped. Her encounter with Ben was short, but she thought he might have some substance to him. How could she be so wrong? He bragged about his conquests and made fun of her all at the same time. Renee no longer had any reason to be guilty regarding her appearance on the show. In fact, now she wanted to get as far as she could in order to give Ben what he deserved...a taste of his own medicine.

# CHAPTER NINE

BEN WATCHED THE show alone. He didn't have any family in town, and his friends would have shot one-liners his way the whole night. When he realized how the crew edited his comments, he nearly called the producer and backed out of the rest of the taping. He came off like a disrespectful, overconfident jerk. The only thing stopping Ben was the fact that he had indeed said the things they aired. Now, he just needed to continue to attempt to change his image and hopefully find the right woman as well.

Ben really experienced something special the night he met the women. The sensation was unlike anything he'd had before. He suspected the electric shock that sprang between him and Renee was static, but he wondered if went further. No one else had shocked him that night, and she had done so in more ways than one. First with her surprising makeup reveal and later with her fire trick. No, Ben most certainly couldn't back out of the show now. He looked forward to what Renee would do next.

THE NEXT MORNING Renee rose earlier than usual to make it to work for the morning show. She was scheduled as a special co-host the day after each *Accept this Dandelion* aired for the duration of the taping. She would update the city on the behind the scenes portions of the broadcast. Renee was nervous. She played off her appearance on the show well in front of her co-workers, but she wasn't sure how the public would react. She was about to find out.

Chuck was live on the air when Renee arrived. He gave her a little wave, and she sat down and made herself comfortable. Renee felt odd being on the other side of the studio behind a microphone atop a smooth counter. She was used to the buttons and faders that usually sat before her during her midday shift. If she happened to win the morning show job, she hoped she and Chuck could alternate duties. She didn't want to lose her abilities at the board. Sitting by and just chiming in on occasion wouldn't be enough for her.

"And next, we have KGBR's very own Renee Lockhart, star of the local TV program *Accept this Dandelion,* in with us to talk about her experience on the show." Chuck started a commercial block, turned his microphone off, and pulled his headphones from his ears. "Good morning." His smile drove his cheeks up higher than Renee had ever see them go. "You're going to be a hit today. I've already taken several calls."

Renee forced a small smile. She hoped Chuck wasn't just being kind. She didn't know what would be worse...callers who wanted to ridicule her, or no callers at all. As the commercials wrapped up, Renee realized she couldn't retreat now. She had to be a guest on the radio program...it was part of heightening her public profile to hopefully get the job in the time slot.

"100.4 KGBR with Chuck and Claudia in the morning...as you already know, Claudia is no longer with us, but we hope to soon

[49]

find her replacement." Chuck paused and started the dramatic music from *Accept this Dandelion* behind his voice. "With us today is the one and only Renee Lockhart, one of twelve women vying for the heart of the city's bachelor, Ben McConnell. We'll be taking your calls all morning long. Think about what questions or comments you might have for Renee, but first, I get a shot at her." Chuck threw his head back and laid out one of his signature laughs. Renee often overheard listeners comment on Chuck's laugh. She had to admit it was contagious and made her smile no matter how bad her day began. It would make working with him fun, as opposed to her solo gig in the afternoon.

"So, Renee…I have plenty of questions, but what I want to talk about more than anything is how in the world did you set yourself on fire? Talk about a bad first date, huh?"

Renee stared at Chuck. She figured those questions would come from the audience, but she never expected Chuck to lob a hardball in her direction. With a swallow, she opened her mouth to answer. They were live, after all, so she couldn't pause more than a second or two or the dead air would reign and kill her rising chances at a job in the top on-air slot. "Well, Chuck." Renee pushed her embarrassment down and summoned up all of her self-deprecation. "When you *really* want to get a man's attention…" She laughed. "I've heard a way to a man's heart is through his stomach, but I finally proved the theory wrong, didn't I? No, it's better to allow the man to be your hero instead. Let him save you. Make him believe you'd simply *die* if he weren't around. Then, you'll know whether or not he likes you. If he isn't into you, he'll just let you go up in flames."

Renee paused and allowed Chuck to throw his head back once more. His laughter quickly caught in the pit of her own stomach, and she laughed at herself along with him.

Chuck wiped his eyes with one finger. "You are too much, Renee," he said. "We have so many calls coming in the board is completely lit up. I'd love to hog you all morning, but I think we have to take a call before this phone sets itself on fire. Good morning, KGBR," Chuck said as he punched a button on the board. Taking live calls was risky and not the norm. A lot of times, they would record their conversations and play them back later. But Chuck could pull the best things out of listeners live, and the station manager let him get away with real time calls. Chuck was also quick with the board buttons. If a caller got out of hand, Chuck could mute the call with a flash of his finger and move on so those listening hardly even noticed anything happening.

"Hey, Chuck," a feisty female voice rang over the line. Her voice sounded like it came from a tunnel. She must be driving. "I wanted to call and tell Renee how awesome she did. I mean, all of the other girls were the same. Renee put some spice into it and really stood out. I think if Ben knows what's best for him, he'll choose you next week and leave the rest behind."

Renee's eyebrows rose. "Thank you." She was surprised. Renee expected everyone to mock her, and she was glad the first response was positive.

"Thanks for calling." Chuck quickly changed callers. "KGBR, you're on with Chuck and Renee."

"Morning, Chuck. Hey there, Renee." A deep male voice rang through the headsets in the studio. Chuck tilted his head as the man continued. "I want to tell the woman who just called she's all wrong." Renee took a deep breath. Here it came. "Renee, you don't belong with Ben…you should be with me."

Renee opened her mouth in surprise and let out a nervous laugh as Chuck threw his head back. "Leave your number at our front office," Chuck said. "We'll keep a running list, and Renee can have her own dating show if things don't work out with Ben."

"Oh, no. No." Renee threw her hands in the air. "Chuck, you don't understand. I don't need a whole list. I just need one." Renee giggled and tried to put on a flirtatious air. "Sir, what did you say your name was?"

Chuck laughed again as he disconnected the call. "Not so fast there, little lady. You have a show to do. First you let Ben McConnell dump you. *Then* you can troll for men."

"And what makes you think Mr. McConnell is going to ditch me?" Renee's confidence grew. She was starting to enjoy herself. She would be good at the morning show gig.

"Ah, good point." Chuck started the next song behind their voices. "Very good point. We'll have more with Renee Lockhart about her experiences on *Accept This Dandelion*, but first another song to get your morning rolling." Chuck slid the microphone faders down and turned them off as he yanked his headphones from his ears and placed them around his neck. Renee took hers off and laid them on the counter in front of her.

"You're really good at this," Chuck said. "A natural."

Renee smiled. "I've been in radio for several years now," she said sarcastically. Chuck was the type of person who appreciated someone who didn't take any flak from people, both on and off the air. The two of them would fit as a team because she knew how to give and take.

"Indeed." He shuffled some papers around. "You keep this up, I might put in a word for you with the higher powers." Chuck winked.

Renee shifted in her seat. The comment excited her. Having Chuck's support for the open morning position would be huge.

With a heightened public profile from the TV slot and Chuck on her side, she almost couldn't lose. The job would be hers for the taking.

When Renee left the studio two hours later, she walked on clouds. The rest of the morning went better than the beginning. She had dozens of supporters and only one crank call marriage proposal. That one sounded like a teenage boy who probably had too much time on his hands. The rest of the callers were genuine and enjoyed her on TV. They supported her efforts to find love. They laughed along with her, but no one teased her, and Renee's appearance on TV had already made her public image soar. She endeared herself to the listeners instead of drawing ridicule as she'd feared.

Now Renee had to get through the day and return to the TV studio to continue her journey with Ben and the rest of the ladies. After the first taping, she dreaded going back and making a fool of herself again. But now she realized her TV character was bringing positive feedback. She could go on.

It didn't matter what happened with Ben. He probably didn't care about any of the women beyond their appearances and long legs. She needed to continue to show her personality so the city could see who she was. And with any luck, viewers would fall for her and demand that she become the next co-host on the KGBR's morning show.

# CHAPTER TEN

AFTER LISTENING TO the radio interview, Ben suspected Renee could become the real star of the show. Listeners called in one after another, praising her for her mouse dance, the way she wiped her makeup off to display her true face, and even how she managed to light herself on fire.

That was what the TV audience wanted? They wouldn't want anything to do with him then. Ben wanted to change his public image, but he was perfectly happy turning the spotlight on Renee and letting her bask in its heat for a while. He already lived under a microscope. It was her turn. She would learn soon enough how hard it was to have people watch your every step.

Ben didn't wish anything ill to befall Renee. In fact, he enjoyed her as much as the radio listeners seemed to. But he knew sudden fame could take a toll and people might turn on her at any point. Just look at how news media portrayed him...playboy bachelor...a lady pleaser...and so on. Ben's image was far larger than it should be. In some ways, what they said was true. But there was more to him than the media let people believe. His goal was to show a little bit of depth through the show. If he fell in love at the same time, he would have it all.

Ben hoped the first round of group dates would shed light on the women. He was a harsh judge, and he dismissed the first two women during the initial eliminations without hesitation. What really held his curiosity was the current running between him and Renee. Was it her clumsy endearment? Did she need to be saved, bringing out his knight in shining armor side? She had alluded to as much on the radio. Or could it be something more? No way to be sure…but he intended to find out.

RENEE DRESSED WITH reckless abandon as she prepared for the next taping session. Her instructions read "come as you are," and she planned to do just that. Apparently, the wardrobe would be provided this time. She was curious to find out what they would do and what they would wear. All Renee knew about the next taping was that Ben had dates planned for them. They split the women into two groups of five, and Ben invited Renee's group out the first night. The second group would have a chance the following evening. All of the contestants had instructions to meet at the studio on the third night for eliminations.

Since Renee figured they'd change before their date so she wore her cut-off shorts and a ratty old t-shirt she used for cleaning and errands. She wanted to be relaxed in case they insisted on doing her hair and makeup again before she had to change into whatever glittery cocktail dress they had waiting. Renee liked to be comfortable above all else, and she wanted to remain that way as long as possible.

Renee was finally excited about the show. The public loved her, and she had stayed true to her personality. If she could stay on track, she would accomplish her goals, and the morning show job might be in reach. Renee had a spring in her step as she entered the TV studio. The first taping was nerve wracking since she didn't know what to expect. Now that she had written off falling in love, she could kick back and enjoy it. The dates would likely be fun, and she could have a good time and let the chips fall where they may.

When Renee arrived at the studio, the hair and makeup people asked if she wanted any help instead of insisting. The date was going to be casual so Renee opted to do her own preparations.

Since the date was labeled casual, she pulled her hair back into a ponytail and freed a few wisps around her face. Renee liked having her hair out of the way, and she wanted Ben to be able to see her face. Though he saw quite a bit of it the other night when she wiped away her makeup with his handkerchief, this time, he would see it in its complete natural state.

Renee had to wear a little makeup to keep the producers happy and so she wouldn't appear washed out on TV. She put on light foundation to make her skin tone even on camera. Then she added clear, shiny lip gloss…the only form of enhancement she wore on a regular basis.

Renee didn't see Eva. She must be in the other group. That was disappointing. Eva was the only girl she connected with on the first night. She hoped they would get a chance to speak at the eliminations and catch up on each other's dates.

"Ladies," Mike the producer called from the center of the room. "Your wardrobe has arrived. Choose your attire, and the car will be here to pick you up in a few minutes."

Most of the dates would take place away from the studio with handheld cameras surrounding the action. Renee moved toward the rack near Mike in the center of the room to see what the attire options were. Would they be playing a sport? Enjoying tea in a garden somewhere? As Renee got closer and closer, she squinted. Whatever was on the rack was very very tiny.

Renee elbowed her way through the group of women who gasped in delight at the miniscule pieces of fabric they held up against themselves. Swimsuits.

"You've got to be kidding me." The other women stopped their chatter, their swimsuits in mid-air. "I mean..." Renee pointed to a nearby strip of fabric in a leggy blonde woman's hand. "I think you got the best one." As the women began to move away from the rack, Renee had the rest of the choices to herself. She grabbed one hanger after another, trying to decide which suit provided the most coverage.

Renee wasn't ashamed of her body. She was athletic and fit, especially for someone in radio who had the option of sitting unseen in a studio and eating all day long. But Renee was annoyed by the wardrobe requirement. It matched Ben's playboy persona. Of course he wanted to see the contestants in tiny bikinis. That would help him judge who to keep for the next round. Any woman he dated had to be perfect, right?

Renee shook her head. *What a jerk*. When she went to the pool, she usually wore a two-piece. Granted, a tankini that showed nothing more than a one-piece would, but still. She always wondered how a bikini would look on her, but she didn't want to find out minutes before a date. Going on a date in a bikini was not cool. Especially so early in the relationship. And in front of the entire city.

Renee gave up on the hangers. None of the suits were larger than the handkerchief she tore from Ben's pocket the first night. With a shrug, she ripped a suit from the next hanger she touched and headed to the bathroom to change.

As Renee changed in her own stall, she formed a plan in her head. It would make her stand out, that was for sure. She wasn't going to hang out in a bikini next to an Amazonian goddess, and she didn't want to show that much of herself to any man on a first date. Her plan would allow her to do both at the same time.

Renee smiled and hoped her idea furthered her goals. If the listening audience appreciated her on the last show, they might really get a kick out of this particular episode.


WHEN BEN RECEIVED the information on his first date, he wasn't sure he liked the idea. It wasn't that he didn't want to see the beautiful women in swimsuits, but their appearance might distract him from what he really wanted. Many of the women probably already judged him based on what they had heard in the media. He wanted a chance to see them for who they really were, and the TV station decided to put them in bathing suits and parade them around before him. That would cloud any man's judgment.

Upon signing on for the show, Ben insisted he have control over the bachelorettes they cast, but he hadn't thought to add a clause to include approval of the dates. He wasn't sure hanging out by a pool would help him decide on a woman to marry, but the male side of him wouldn't complain.

Ben arrived on location several minutes before the women. He had on his swim trunks and tank top, and someone offered him a fruity beverage with an umbrella stuck in the side. He took his sunglasses from his pocket and placed them on his face. He was ready.

When the women arrived, Ben knew immediately because the quiet lapping pool water was interrupted by shrills of excitement outside the entrance. Ben stood to await his candidates and watched as they strolled into the deck area. The taping had officially begun.

Ben pasted a smile on his face as one pair of long legs after another walked before him. Luckily for him, they were all wearing cover-ups for the time being. At least he would be able to get in his initial statements before he got tongue-tied.

"Welcome, ladies." Ben raised his drink as they stood in a line before him. "I appreciate you joining me for a relaxing day by the water. Today, I really want to kick back and get to know all of you. And hey, if we can fit a little water volleyball into the day, even better." Ben lowered his glasses on his nose. "What do you say we get this party started?"

The women clapped and cheered as Ben looked slowly from one to another. When he got to the end of the line, he noticed Renee, clapping in a lackluster manner. Ben frowned. What was she hiding under her cover-up?

One by one the women began to do just as Ben imagined…take off their cover-ups to reveal tiny bikinis that shimmered and glowed in all the right places. Ben knew if he wasn't used to beautiful women already, he would have a hard time keeping his jaw in place and his wits about him.

Instead of jumping straight into the water, beautiful bikini-clad women surrounded him. He wasn't sure what to do. He glanced over their heads when he realized one was missing. Renee stood in place, playing with the bottom of her cover-up.

"Excuse me, ladies." Ben patted one woman on the shoulder while gently pushing another aside. "I'll be right back with you." He swiftly walked over to Renee, a camera close at his back.

"Renee." He lifted a fruity drink in her direction. "Won't you join us? You look rather hot and alone over here."

"Thanks," Renee replied sarcastically. She had to know Ben wasn't trying to compliment her appearance. As Ben got closer, he examined her a little more. All of the women wore their hair long and flowing, showing off every angle of what they had to offer. Renee, on the other hand, had her hair bunched up on the back of her head in a ponytail. And Ben had to admit, she had a fresh and pretty face.

"Don't you want to swim?" Ben asked, letting his eyes rake down Renee's body. Was she ever going to come out of the cover-up?

Renee shrugged. "I will if you will," she said. And with a swift motion and a lot of power, Ben found himself falling backward into the water. He sputtered and kicked and made his way back to the top, his fruity drink littering the clean water with red. He grabbed the small umbrella floating nearby and swam to the edge of the pool.

Renee had taken her cover-up off, but what she had underneath was nothing like what the studio provided. Instead of a bikini or even a one piece, she wore old cut-off shorts and a ratty t-shirt. Before he could scold her for pushing him in, she took a flying leap over his head and did a cannonball right behind him in the center of the pool.

Ben swam over to where Renee landed as if he was being pulled to her like a current. The other women watched them from the edge of the water. Before Renee surfaced, Ben caught her around the waist and pulled her against him.

"You know you're going to have to pay for that," Ben said quietly.

"Just trying to cool you off." She wiped her hands over her hair, slicking it back into her ponytail.

"After the fire the other night?" he teased.

"After the fire today." Renee looked at the nearby waiting women.

Ben followed her gaze and laughed. They certainly were a hot bunch, he had to agree.

"What are you wearing anyway?" Ben knew their time was running out.

"A bikini just like them."

Ben frowned and grasped the corner of her ratty shirt in his hand.

"No one said we couldn't wear anything else." Renee pushed her feet against his legs and freed herself from his grasp.

Ben shivered despite the warm water surrounding him. So she was wearing a bathing suit underneath her clothing. She was teasing him...for sure. She must be the type of woman who wanted to draw a man in only to push him away. He would have to be careful with her. The other women were slowly lowering themselves into the pool, taking precautions to keep their hair dry. They weren't leaving anything to the imagination. Ben would be much better off with one of them.

# *CHAPTER ELEVEN*

THE BEGINNING OF the date went better than Renee expected. She didn't plan on pushing Ben into the pool, but he was asking for it. The way he stood so close to the edge with his little drink, trying to ogle her through her cover-up to see what she had to offer underneath it. He deserved what he got...and more.

Renee enjoyed the rest of the afternoon. A pool volleyball game broke out and Renee found herself on the opposite side of the net as Ben. It was her against Ben because the other women moved slowly to avoid getting their hair and makeup wet. Renee also wondered if they restricted their motions so nothing would pop out of their tiny tops.

Renee was glad on more than one occasion that she covered up the bikini she wore with her regular clothing. She was comfortable in the water, out of the pool and everywhere in between. After the volleyball game, Ben took the women to the side one by one. Instead of lying by the pool and sunning herself like the others, Renee played.

She swam a few laps, but once she got tired, she did handstands to see how long she could hold her feet in the air. When she no longer thought she could outdo her time, she did flips in the water. It reminded her of swimming as a child and though she was alone in the pool, she was having a blast. Renee had goals for the experience, but life was short, and she decided to have as much fun as possible.

As the date neared its end, and the sun began to dip below the horizon, Renee wondered if she would get another chance to speak with Ben. She didn't really care other than the fact that wherever Ben went, the cameras followed. If she wanted more screen time to make an impression on the audience, she would have to spend time with him.

Renee finally got out of the water, and a chill ran down her spine. She wrapped a big white towel around her shoulders. She was going to have to ride back to the studio and then drive home in the clothes she was wearing, and she wanted to dry off.

"Renee." A voice called her from the other side of the pool. She glanced up. Ben beckoned her. So that's how he got his women. He made a little hand gesture and expected them to follow orders. Renee wiped her face dry as she scoffed. She'd go to him because this was a TV show, but if he had any illusions of having her in his life, he would have to work harder.

Renee walked around the pool, holding the towel tightly. Ben stood when she approached and gestured toward the chair across from him. As soon as Renee sat down, she noticed cameras staring at her.

"You seemed to have a fun day." Ben gestured toward the water. Renee wondered if he caught glimpses of her antics while he spoke with the other women.

"You too." Renee directed her gaze across the pool at the bikini clad women who finally started to put their cover-ups back on.

"You cold?" Ben scooted his chair closer to hers.

Renee shivered. "No." She would have bet big money he used that particular line several other times during the date to get his hands on half-naked women. It wouldn't work on her.

"Of course not. Okay, Renee. I'm going to ask. Why are you wearing that?"

Renee looked down at the towel. Her cut-off shorts peaked out beneath it.

"Have you ever gone on a first date in a Speedo?" Renee asked in a matter-of-fact voice.

"A Speedo? Why in the world..."

"Exactly," Renee said. "Why would you do that? And yet you expected us to do virtually the same thing while you sat here in your comfy shorts and tank top. The producer said the date was casual. Sitting around in something that looked like underwear didn't seem casual to me. So I wore what did."

Ben held up his hands in surrender. "Okay. You win."

Renee nodded her head and shivered again. The temperature was dropping along with the sun. It took all of her strength to keep her teeth from chattering. Renee enjoyed letting Ben know what she thought about his pool party. She hoped the women in the city agreed. Surely most of them felt objectified at some point in their lives, and the fact that she wasn't going to stand for it put them on her side.

"You're really something." Ben looked across the space separating them.

Renee warmed instantly as she caught his gaze. He looked into her eyes and time stopped. Without any explanation at all, a current ran through her body, much like the one she experienced the other night when his touch sent a real static shock up her arm. This time, they weren't even touching.

Renee involuntarily shivered a third time for a whole different reason.

"You're definitely cold." Ben stood and grabbed Renee by the shoulders to lift her from her chair. "Here." He wrapped his arms around her and pulled her face against his chest. "This is probably the last thing you want, but I'm not going to let you freeze to death before my eyes."

Renee grasped the towel in her hands, squeezing it so tightly she thought her knuckles might burst. She wasn't sure what to do. She couldn't hug him back because her arms were trapped in front of her. She also wasn't able push him again. Her face was turned the opposite direction from the other women so she couldn't even see their reactions to the embrace.

"Remember what I said," Ben whispered against her ear. "I'm not putting the fire out this time."

Renee knew there wasn't a real fire around all the water. As she shivered a final time, she knew it wasn't from the cold…but rather the heat between them. She looked up at Ben, finding her nose near his chin. As he gazed down at her, she had the sudden urge to raise herself to her toes and kiss him.

Renee turned to the side slightly. Before she gave in to that crazy notion, she had to get out of there. Sure, Ben smelled great despite the chlorine tinge and looked even better, but he was a womanizer, and he would never change. He was working his magic on her. He probably saw her as a challenge. Men liked the chase.

"All better," Renee said as she twisted from his grip, anxious to get away from his burning brown eyes and his hot flesh. If Ben wanted a chase, she'd give it to him. But instead of letting him catch her, she planned to keep running…as fast as she could.

# CHAPTER TWELVE

RENEE DIDN'T LIKE the way her mind kept wandering to Ben, and the fact that she still felt his tan arms around her. She wasn't sure what bothered her more, the idea that Ben might actually be interested in her or the thought that he had an effect on her. Renee sat down in front of her home computer. She needed to forget Ben's second group date, scheduled to happen later. Why should she care? He was a womanizing jerk. But Eva would be on the date, and she didn't want the sweet girl to be swept up by the excitement.

Renee curled her fingers over the keyboard. She didn't go back to work until after the elimination ceremony the following night, so in the meantime she'd write a few scripts from home. She told her boss she would do as much as possible to help out in her absence, and the sales people took her up on the offer by sending her plenty of commercials to write.

The first script was for a heating and cooling company. They wanted to advertise special deals to listeners who regularly got their HVAC equipment checked out. An incentive for loyal customers. Renee thought for a minute. Heating...cooling. She began to type.

*House on ice in the winter and on fire in the summer?* Renee paused. As soon as she typed the word 'fire' her mind immediately flew back to Ben's burning eyes boring a hole right through her own. From there, she began to think about his warm skin next to hers and then she moved on to the night they first met when she actually set herself on fire.

Renee pushed back from her computer abruptly. She needed to stay away from anything related to fire...even the simple word. She cranked her air conditioning down a few degrees and decided she would put her writing off until she could think straight. Maybe once the eliminations were over her head would work better. Ben would probably cut her out, and she could resume her everyday normal life. If by some miracle he kept her, seeing him again would send any romantic thoughts fleeing quickly.

Renee admitted she found him attractive. And what was wrong with that? His handsome features included eyes that could drill through wood, much less into a woman's heart. His hair appeared light and soft. Any woman had to find it nearly impossible not to run her fingers through it. But exterior attraction was one thing. Renee needed a *whole* lot more in a man. She wanted inner beauty as well. Something Ben certainly lacked.

Renee smiled, she was putting her thoughts of Ben behind her for the moment. He was gorgeous, but his appeal began and ended there. The women he was taking out that evening could have him. Renee wouldn't give him another thought until he stood before her with dandelions in his hands.

BEN RAN HIS hand through his hair. His second group date promised to be as intense as the first. The producer wanted to be fair. Every woman would have a chance to flaunt herself in a bikini. How shallow did the TV staff think he was? They must believe he needed to see nearly every inch of a woman before deciding whether or not she was right for him.

The second date would take place on the beach. Not by the ocean since they weren't anywhere near one, but rather, beside a local lake. Ben arrived well before the women. They had to report to the studio and get dressed first. He wondered if they would be offered the same skimpy bikinis from the day before.

Ben gazed out over the lake and watched children play on a playground nearby. He thought about Renee. She was the only woman who hadn't taken advantage of the chance to show off her body. They'd been close a few times. He knew she had a nice figure. But even though she was in shape and could have stood up next to any of the other women on the date, she stayed fully covered.

He smiled as he thought about her in her shirt and shorts, a sore thumb among the beauties swarming around him. But Ben knew what it was like to have a sore thumb. Such an injury caused him to baby that digit…favor it, even. He had to wonder if that was why he seemed to favor Renee. Was he sorry for her? Was she the underdog he couldn't help but root for? He wasn't sure, but she had something different.

The nearby children continued to play as Ben made a decision no one would believe. It was obvious he was being treated a certain way because of how people perceived him. This show might help him find love, but it was also a great way to get in front of the public eye. This was his chance to show the city his true character.

RENEE'S NERVES COURSED through her body. Her dress that evening fit in better with the other contestants. For once, she didn't want to stand out. She wanted to blend in, hear Ben's decision, and head home. Then she could spend the rest of the evening trying to think up witty things to say on the radio the next morning in regards to her dismissal.

When Renee first found out she got cast on the show, she went through the back of her closet. She had a few items she thought she could wear, and the dress chosen for that night was one of them. She wore it to homecoming the year she and her friend Jay attended together. Jay, the type of friend all the girls loved, went to so many school dances he actually bought a tux in order to stop renting them. He was the stand-in date for any girl without a boyfriend. And he was the best date every girl had. That year, Renee wore a long red dress she found on the rack at a teen store in the mall. Why she still had it, she didn't know, but the fact it still fit made her proud, even though it was tight in a few places. If Renee was careful about how she moved and breathed, she should be fine.

As the participants gathered for the second round of eliminations, Renee watched the room carefully. She wanted to try and predict what would happen based on how the women acted. She already figured herself in for one elimination, but could she choose the other woman Ben might dump on TV? Renee looked from one woman to another. They all appeared about the same. Their short dresses glittered under the studio lights, and their excited faces told Renee they certainly didn't think they would go home.

"Renee." Eva called from behind her. Renee turned and lightly embraced her. They hadn't spent much time together, but they were both on the crazy show. They might even become friends after. Eva was the only one who seemed to understand Renee on a different level.

"How was your date?" Renee asked. She hadn't heard anything about the other date. She wanted news. She would have to discuss as much as possible on the morning show, and she wanted to get behind the scenes scoop that wouldn't air.

"Crazy." Eva shook her shimmering dark hair.

Renee stared for a moment, mesmerized by her beauty. "How so?" she finally asked. "What did you do?"

"Well..." Eva pulled Renee over to the stiff couch in the center of the set. "We were supposed to have an old fashioned beach party down by the lake. You know, cocktails, sunscreen, beach volleyball, the whole bit."

"Let me guess, bikinis were involved."

Eva held a hand over her mouth to stifle a giggle. "Oh, yes. A whole rack of them right over there." She pointed across the room to the area Renee remembered seeing the bathing suits. "And we all put them on, along with a cover-up, but you'll never guess what happened when we got to the beach."

"What?"

"Ben waited for us and once we lined up in front of him, he took off his sunglasses and asked us to leave the cover-ups on."

Renee squinted at Eva. Her eyes glittered under the studio light, and Renee wasn't sure she heard her right. "He what?"

Eva nodded. "He wanted to play Frisbee instead of volleyball, and he said everyone would be more comfortable throwing themselves into the game. He indicated he didn't think we would be able to enjoy playing in bathing suits so he encouraged us to keep our outer wear on."

Renee blinked. Ben hadn't wanted the second group of women to reveal their bikinis? What, had he seen too much the day before?

"It was actually sweet," Eva said. "Like he was thinking of our dignity and putting us before the show."

Renee tilted her head. Why hadn't Ben said anything on her date? She might have avoided standing out as she had.

"Not everyone listened, and some of the girls still took their cover-ups off. But Ben was right—those who did certainly didn't play Frisbee to the best of their ability like the rest of us. I mean, who wants to go diving into the sand when you don't know what might pop out of where."

Renee laughed and tried to picture them playing in their bathing suits, catching the Frisbee in one hand and holding their bikinis in place with the other one.

"Tell me about your date. How did it go?"

Renee raised an eyebrow. "Well, there were bikinis. And somehow I managed to push Ben into the pool."

"You didn't." Eva clasped Renee's hands.

"I did, and I don't regret it for a second."

Eva giggled again, but both women quickly silenced as the producer clomped to the center of the room and called for their attention.

"Ladies. We're going to start taping shortly. Do your interview with the cameras on the sides of the set as before and line up in two rows. Ben will make an announcement followed by the elimination. You won't talk to him before the ceremony. He says he's made up his mind, and we have plenty of footage from the dates to cover the hour."

The producer stomped away, and Renee squeezed Eva's hands. "Here goes nothing." The women stood and got in line for their interviews.

BEN PACED IN the green room off to the side of the set. He heard the nervous chatter beyond the wall. The time to tell the contestants what he decided about eliminations was near. He practiced what he wanted to say and wondered about their reaction...as well as the reaction from the TV crew.

Before he could re-think his speech, he took a deep breath, straightened his shirt and tie, and walked out onto the set.

As soon as Ben situated himself before the women, the room fell silent. The cameras whirred around him.

He cleared his throat. "Good evening." He was nervous for the first time. He caught Renee's eye and gave her a slight smile. He had her to thank. Her antics inspired him to allow his real character to shine through. "Tonight, ladies, I want to share what I want in a wife."

The women shifted, and a few looked at one another, but most simply smiled and gazed at Ben.

"I want you to know that I think you are gorgeous." Ben looked directly at Eva, the most beautiful without a doubt. "Your beauty humbles me, and I am grateful any of you would even consider dating me." Ben bowed his head for a moment before continuing. "But what you need to understand is though I see your beauty, it only goes so far." Ben paused again, placing his hand over his heart. "What I want is here." He tapped his fingers, hoping the women would get what he was saying. He wanted them to know they were pretty, but he needed something deeper. He desired inner beauty. He didn't want them to try so hard to impress him. He wanted them to be themselves. He thought his speech along with his first selection would give them the idea.

Ben held a dandelion up in front of him, its yellow face standing at attention. "Renee." He searched the women until he found her. He registered her shock as she stepped around the group and made her way across the set toward him.

Once she stood right in front of him, Ben continued. "Renee, will you accept this dandelion?"

Renee frowned. "Did you mean what you said?"

Ben nodded. "With all my heart."

Renee threw her arms around Ben's neck and squeezed him tightly.

Ben wasn't sure what surprised him more…the fact that Renee threw herself at him or the ripping sound.

Renee froze as Ben wrapped his hands behind her back to reciprocate the hug. It was Ben's turn to frown as his hands met bare skin instead of satin fabric.

"Um…" Ben realized what happened as the women tittered behind Renee.

"I'll accept your dandelion," Renee muttered into his ear, "if you get me out of here. Now."

Ben held Renee's back with one hand and pushed her gently behind him. No cameras hid back there. "Excuse me for a moment ladies." He backed out of the room, keeping Renee's bare back hidden with his own.

Once on the side of the set, Renee wrenched her arm around herself and grasped at the sides of her broken zipper. Ben watched, amused.

"Thanks," Renee mumbled.

"My pleasure. I really did mean what I said." He placed his finger below Renee's chin and raised her eyes to meet his. "I'm looking for what's in here." He put his hand on her chest where her heart would be.

"I could tell," Renee replied. "And I'm sorry in advance."

# CHAPTER THIRTEEN

RENEE WANTED TO explain herself a little more, but before she opened her mouth, Mike, the producer, gave Ben a hard shove.

"Get back out there." He shot Renee a scathing stare. "You can stay here." He guided Ben out in front of the other ladies.

Renee watched backstage as Ben continued on with the dandelion ceremony. She smiled at the crushed dandelion in her hand as she held her dress together with the other.

Renee tried to let herself enjoy the moment instead of dwelling on what went wrong. Ben seemed to be genuine, and he was trying to tell the women he didn't want them to overdo it. He wanted a real woman with inner beauty and not someone superficial. Renee could fall for a man like that. She tightened her grip on the dandelion. The very first one he handed out.

As much as she wanted to, Renee couldn't dwell on the positive aspects of the evening. Just before the elimination ceremony, she did an interview on camera…and the things she said about Ben had not been kind. Oh, and her dress tore up her back, allowing a cool breeze to give her a chill.

Renee took in the rest of the dandelion ceremony out of sight. The whole thing was ridiculous. Here was the most eligible man in the city handing out a bunch of weeds to women with smiles plastered on their faces. What made him do this show in the first place?

She looked at her own dandelion, its bloom no longer standing at the end of the stem, but rather laying on top of her hand and beginning to brown. She planned to keep the weed. Maybe sell it on eBay later. For whatever reason, she had saved the other one too.

Renee wanted to talk to Ben as soon as possible. If they aired the things she said, she may fall from his good graces. She wanted to explain she judged him too quickly...and too harshly. She only hoped he would understand and give her another chance.

RENEE REFUSED JANICE'S offer to hold a second viewing party. The pressure was too large. Watching herself in front of all those people was embarrassing. Janice relented, but only since Renee promised to come over and view the program with her. Renee didn't want to be alone for the event. She needed someone to help her process everything and Janice might have some insight into the ordeal.

As she settled into Janice's comfy couch, she thought about the way Ben's hands warmed her bare skin. She didn't like that her dress split, and she hoped the editing eliminated that portion of the program from viewers. But Renee had to admit, she liked his warm palms on her back.

She smiled. She might still come off as the strange one in the bunch, but it wouldn't be as bad as lighting herself on fire.

Janice plopped down next to her with a large bowl of popcorn. She threw a few kernels into her mouth. "Any details you want to spill before it starts?" she asked expectantly.

"Hmm." Renee thought with care. Saying too much might ruin the show's outcome for Janice, but she could drop a few hints to wet her appetite. "Let's just say I showed him my backside."

"You what?" Janice raised her eyebrows.

Renee winked at her as the show's music ramped up on the screen. "Just wait."

Together, they listened to the announcer explain the situation as well as the dates that would take place on the program. "And later," he said, "we will find out if the women Ben chooses accept his dandelions."

Renee rolled her eyes. She hoped she wasn't coming off cheesy like the announcer.

Janice tensed beside her as the contestants walked out to the pool one by one in their cover-ups. Janice applauded loudly as Renee appeared, but quieted to listen when the bachelor gave his speech. As the ladies peeled off their cover-ups and the camera zoomed in for close-ups, Janice shot Renee a look. "I can't believe you're going to show the goods on TV."

Renee smiled secretively, her eyes glued to the screen as she pushed Ben into the pool. A few moments later, she revealed her shirt and shorts.

Janice threw her head back and laughed. "Deserved that, didn't he?"

Renee anticipated the second portion of the dates. She only heard a little about it from Eva, and she wanted to see the expression on Ben's face when he asked the women to keep their clothes on. Renee leaned forward and watched the second date unfold. Everything Eva said was true. Ben treated them like real ladies. Renee wished she had seen that side of him on her date. Maybe she wouldn't have said what she did to the camera before the elimination.

The commercial break gave Janice and Renee a chance to decompress and discuss.

"How in the world did you manage getting out of that?" Janice turned to Renee with a sparkle in her eye. "Not only did you avoid the bikini brigade, but you did so with style. And I think you even got his attention."

"A ton of water rushing toward you unrepentantly will do that." Renee remembered the look on Ben's face when she shoved him into the pool.

"Indeed. Okay, girl, you absolutely have to tell me. Did you get a dandelion? Is this the end of the road for you or not?"

Renee shook her head as the show started again. Instead of the elimination ceremony, they showed clips of the interviews from participants. Eva began. "Ben is a dream. He treats us with such respect, the way all men should. There's something about him…he's really special."

Eva had a far off look in her eyes. She wondered if her newfound friend was falling for Ben. She hoped she didn't get hurt in this process.

"He's totally hot," Clara said. Renee remembered her as the long-legged blonde. "I can't get enough of him and hope I never have to say goodbye."

The interviews went on and on. When Renee's face came onto the screen, she shuddered.

"Ben really got what he deserved this week. His ego needed a good dunking. I mean, he had us all in bathing suits in no time flat. If that's the kind of man they pick to be the bachelor, I'd love to see those in their discard pile." Renee scoffed and rolled her eyes on camera.

"Oh, snap." Janice reached for some popcorn.

Renee was grateful they hadn't shown more. She said quite a bit, and they edited her down to a few nasty comments. If they had shown any more, she would have come off even worse towards Ben.

Renee sat back in the couch and watched as the elimination ceremony began. It was interesting that they moved from her interview right into Ben's speech. He spoke eloquently about wanting the women to be themselves with him. It was such a change from the way Renee made him sound.

Then, without hesitation, he handed the first dandelion over to Renee. Janice jumped into the air, not taking her eyes from the screen. Her shout covered the sound of Renee's dress ripping, but not the surprise on Renee's face. Janice cackled as Renee whispered into Ben's ear, and he quickly escorted her off the stage.

The camera zoomed in on the remaining women's faces. "Wardrobe malfunction." Tracy shook her bright red curls and giggled.

"How embarrassing," Clara added. Eva looked genuinely sorry for Renee, but she was the only one who didn't thoroughly enjoy the situation.

A few moments later, Ben returned, glancing over his shoulder to the side of the set where Renee stood. He proceeded to hand out the rest of the dandelions, including one for Eva.

Renee was glad Eva would continue on the show, but she hoped she avoided getting hurt. Maybe she was the one for Ben. It would be a good outcome. Now that Renee was starting to really believe Ben might not be such a bad guy, perhaps he could end up with someone nice. Before, she'd have put him with Clara or one of the other superficial women.

"You did it!" Janice exclaimed. "You're still on. And boy, I think he might just have a thing for you…calling you first and all."

Renee smiled. "I think he wants to see what I'll do next."

"Well, yeah, keep a man guessing, and he'll always come back for more." Janice scraped the last of the popcorn from the bottom of the bowl. "What comes next?"

"Eight women are left so group dates will continue. I'll be on the second date this time, and eliminations will be the night after that." If by some miracle she survived, the one-on-one dates came next, along with two on one and other varieties of dates.

"You have got to hang on," Janice encouraged. "This is too good to pass up."

Renee agreed on her way out the door. Janice's comment could mean a number of things. She was getting her name out there...she was very entertaining to watch...and Ben might be more than she bargained for.


THE NEXT MORNING, Renee arrived at the radio station bright and early. Her eyes were heavy because getting to sleep the night before had been impossible. She kept wondering how Ben took the comments she made about him and whether or not he regretted giving her a dandelion.

"Morning, TV star," Chuck greeted as she entered the studio.

"Hardy har." Renee kept her head down.

"That was quite a show last night," he said, trying to engage her.

Renee nodded. She wanted to save everything for the listening audience.

"You ready to go on?" Chuck's excitement rose as the song ended, and he got ready to turn the microphones on.

"Ready as I'll ever be." Renee faked a smile in hopes of it permeating through to her attitude.

"Goooood morning, you're listening to 100.4 KGBR with Chuck and Claudia in the morning. Claudia, as you know, is out, but we'll have a replacement for her soon."

Renee's heart beat faster in her chest. That was the whole reason she allowed herself to be signed up for the show in the first place...her hope of taking over Claudia's old job. Somehow, she seemed to lose sight of the initial goal.

"With us this morning is our very own Renee Lockhart, co-star of *Accept this Dandelion.*" Chuck drummed his fingers on the counter before him. "And, I'm happy to say, she will be continuing on with the show...at least for another week. But, Renee, I have to ask, do you even want to go on? I mean, come on...push the guy into the pool, talk about him behind his back...of course, then he saved your back, am I right?"

Renee laughed, not altogether pleased that Chuck brought up her dress mishap. Too late now. She had to roll with it.

"Well, Chuck," Renee began, "I should have known better. I mean, I hadn't worn the dress since high school."

"Is that right?" Chuck asked before immediately steering Renee back to the original topic. "Dress aside, what is Ben really like? Did you mean what you said about him?"

"Oh, I meant it." Renee saw her chance to make amends before the public. "But people can change their opinions at the drop of a hat, and I'm glad to say, I already have."

"You mean you said those things and meant them, but you have since changed your mind?"

"That's right, Chuck. I mean, how would you take it if you went on a date with a girl who just wanted you to take your shirt off?"

"That's my kind of date." Chuck guffawed.

"Okay, okay," Renee conceded. "But you understand what I mean."

Chuck sighed. "I suppose I do. You're saying you thought Ben was objectifying you and the other women."

"Exactly. And that's why I made the comments I did."

"So what changed your mind?"

"Well..." Renee shrugged. "It wasn't any one thing. Another contestant told me details regarding the second date, and it sounded like Ben had a completely different attitude that day. And then what he said at the elimination ceremony really got to me."

"The stuff about the heart?" Chuck mock sniffled into the microphone and wiped a fake tear from beneath his eye. "That was beautiful. You're right."

Renee sighed. She was being serious. "I know it may sound cheesy, but I think he meant it. And I'm happy to say whether I'm the girl for him or not, I am excited to move on and find out."

"You sound like you're in it to win it," Chuck said with surprise.

"I'm single...he's single..." Renee tried to lighten the mood. "We'll see what happens."

"That we will. I'm sorry we have to wait a whole week to find out. In the meantime, when you notice dandelions by the side of the road, say a little prayer for Renee. No offense, Lockhart, but I think you're going to need all the help you can get."

"None taken...and I agree."

Chuck wrapped up the talk break and started another song. After he turned the microphones off and pulled the headphones from his ears, he stood.

"Renee, man, you really know what you're doing."

Renee's heart quickened again. Was Chuck complimenting her on her radio abilities? "Thanks, Chuck." She hoped he would indicate his plans to recommend her for the morning show job opposite him.

"I mean, you are playing hard to get like none other. Push the man in the pool...insult him on TV...what more can you possibly do to the guy?"

Renee forced a laugh. Chuck was still talking about the dating show. "I guess we'll see, Chuck. Time will tell."

# CHAPTER FOURTEEN

HALF A WEEK had passed since the last show aired, and Ben was beside himself. He couldn't stop second-guessing his choices. Going into the elimination ceremony, he wanted to keep Renee around longer. She intrigued him and kept him guessing. He never knew what she would do, and he liked that. More than anything else, she was real, and she didn't try too hard to impress him.

But it didn't matter what Ben thought about Renee. Love was a two way street and after hearing her comments regarding him, he wasn't positive she liked him.

Ben refused to listen to her on the radio the next morning. He didn't need to be lambasted in public again. The only reason he wanted to see her again at all was to make sure she understood who was in charge. If he fell in love on the silly show, he needed it to be with someone who loved him back. And if Renee didn't think it even slightly possible, she needed to step up and say so. She accepted his dandelions, and as ridiculous as it sounded, that should mean something.

As Ben prepared for the next round of dates, he steeled himself against the women. He sensed many of them weren't there for the right reasons. Some appeared in hopes of local fame while others wanted a little fun. This week Ben promised to weed those women out. If all they wanted was his money and what he could do for them, they should go back to wherever they came from. He wasn't up to games any longer.

RENEE KNEW THIS particular date was the most important thus far in the process. What Ben thought of her mattered. Of course, it made a difference all along in terms of whether or not she would stay on the show, but now, Renee really wanted him to recognize who she was.

So far, he'd seen a prankster who lit herself on fire, pushed him into pools, ripped open her dress, danced like a maniac, and talked bad about him behind his back. Renee hoped more than anything that Ben listened to her on the radio the morning after the last show aired. It was a long shot, but her comments there would help her case.

Ben had been on a date the day before, and Renee heard nothing about it. She hoped she would get some details from someone so she wouldn't be surprised when the show aired. But for now, she needed to concentrate on her own date.

The four contestants going on the date were told to wear casual clothing, and as Renee glanced around the sparsely lit studio where the women gathered, she realized casual meant unique things to different people. Clara had on the shortest shorts humanly possible to accentuate her mile-long legs while Tracy had on a mini-dress and high heels. Renee wore jeans and a decent top. She was glad when Eva walked into the room with jeans on as well, though she had on heels.

"I'm so happy to see a friend on this date." Renee watched Clara and Tracy check themselves out in the nearby mirror.

"They're definitely in a different league." Eva glanced over at the other women.

"The outer space one." Renee laughed as Eva grabbed her arm and nodded in agreement.

Mike, the producer, entered the studio and garnered the women's attention with a sound snap of his clipboard. "Ladies. Today you will be driving so I hope you're comfortable." He gave Tracy and Clara the once over as he continued. "Before you take the shuttle to the sight of the shoot, I'd like a word with you, Renee."

"Oo, you're in trouble," Eva cooed as Renee followed Mike off the small set.

Mike turned to her in a dark corner of the set. "Renee, I need to know what to expect from you."

"Excuse me?" Renee frowned.

Mike sighed. "We will be around high-powered vehicles today. If there are going to be any fires, I need to have the right crews on hand."

Renee raised her eyebrows. "Are you serious? I don't light fires for fun. I didn't set anything at all on fire last week." She realized how silly her statement sounded.

Mike nodded. "True, true, but a lot worse can go wrong in a car."

"Worse than catching fire?"

"Maybe not."

"Look, I think you and I got off on the wrong foot, Mike," Renee said with sincerity. She knew Mike had Ben's ear, and if she wanted to fix the impression she made on Ben, she needed to start over with Mike as well. "I apologize for any havoc I created. I haven't meant to cause trouble."

"You didn't mean to push our bachelor into the pool?"

Renee sighed. "That I meant. But I didn't intend to start any fires, and I certainly don't want to do any harm."

Mike glanced down at his clipboard. "Just be careful, okay?"

"With the cars?" Renee sensed the change in Mike's mood.

"With Ben," he replied before he rushed off to corral the women for the shuttle.

RENEE DIDN'T HAVE much time to think about what Mike meant because the ride to the track was short, and Eva talked next to her the whole drive. Once they arrived, Renee realized they really would be driving. A few small cars lined the track, and the smell of fresh dirt hung in the air. They were going to race.

The only race Renee had ever been in involved go-carts. This was more serious, but she could handle it. After all, she regularly went above the speed limit on the interstate...to keep up with traffic, of course.

Clara teetered on her high heels, and Tracy pulled at her short skirt. They might not be comfortable in their chosen casual attire. Renee was glad she wore her sneakers and jeans.

When Ben arrived in a racing jumpsuit, all of Renee's thoughts regarding everyone's attire vanished. The suit hugged Ben in all the right places, and the helmet beneath his arm made him appear slightly dangerous. Something about danger drew a woman to a man.

"Good afternoon, ladies." Ben gave a little bow. "Thank you for coming today. It's only right to inform you of what happened yesterday."

Renee squinted into the sun. Ben's date with the other four contestants. She was curious about what they did, but since he didn't usually share details, she was surprised he would spill any now.

"Yesterday I went on a date with the other four participants left on the show," Ben continued. "But I had an awakening of sorts, and before the date began, I asked each of them to leave."

Renee blinked as Tracy gasped beside her.

"It came to my attention that some of the women who auditioned for the show didn't come to find love." Ben looked at each of the ladies in turn. Renee squirmed when his gaze fell to her face. Was he talking to her? Did he know about the radio gig she wanted to secure? "I realize fame and fortune are tempting, but I want each of you to understand those things are icing on the cake."

Renee checked the row of women. There was really only four of them left?

"And I, as corny as it sounds, am the cake."

Clara giggled, and Renee attempted to stifle her own laughter.

"What I'm saying is I want you to be here because you want *me* and not something I can offer you. If any of you have dreams of riches, you may as well leave now."

The silence permeated the air as Ben inspected the row of contestants again.

"Yesterday, I gave the women the same out I offer you. One of them took it. She was the only honest one in the bunch. I may not know you ladies well, but I knew enough about those on the date yesterday to realize what they wanted. One of the things they didn't want was to fall in love with me for who I am."

Renee squirmed. She certainly didn't plan to leave on her own, but Ben might force her to go if she didn't admit her reasons for auditioning.

"I sense more honesty from the group we have here today." Ben paused, his gaze on Eva. "Each of you has shown me a true side to yourself, and that gives me hope for a relationship and a future."

Renee pictured Clara and Tracy standing beside her. She couldn't believe she was in the same category as those two. What had they shown him other than their bikini-clad bodies? Now certainly wasn't the time for jealousy.

"I asked each of you to accept a dandelion at the last elimination ceremony, and I meant it." Ben shifted his helmet to his other arm. "If your opinion of me doesn't measure up, I would ask that you simply own up to it." He stared at Renee.

Renee took a step forward. She didn't know what she would say, but she had to make a move.

"There…there's something I need to tell you," she stuttered. Renee knew she needed to clear the air between them faster than the race cars sitting nearby. If she didn't, she might be gone in sixty seconds…or less.

Ben jerked his head to the left, and Renee followed his lead. They walked silently to a small alcove beneath the stands where spectators would go to get refreshments during an event. Once out of view, Renee exhaled. The camera that followed them eyed her closely. There was no turning back.

"I need to apologize." Renee lifted her eyes to meet Ben's. "I'm sure you watched last week's show, and you heard a few things come from my mouth that weren't exactly complimentary."

Ben scoffed. Renee knew she deserved any cynicism he had to offer.

"I am no different than the women you sent home yesterday." Renee meant it in more than one way. "I judged you before the tapings started. I had my ideas about you, and I didn't give you a chance to prove yourself before I made up my mind."

Renee searched his face. She couldn't be sure, but she thought he almost looked amused. She decided to forge ahead.

"Ben, I really appreciated what you said at the last dandelion ceremony. I realized how wrong I was to jump to conclusions. Even though everything you did up to that point backed up what I thought…I think I was seeing what I wanted to see. And now, well, I *want* to see something different, and I believe what I'm starting to see is much more in line with who you really are."

Ben's look turned to one of confusion. Renee couldn't blame him. She was talking in circles and moving her hands around just as fast.

"What I'm trying to say," she went on, doing her best to get her point across and glancing over at the intruding camera, "is I do really want to be here. I honestly don't know what might be between us, but I hope to find out. You must be angry with me, and I completely understand. But no matter what I said or did before, I truly want to get to know you for you." Renee found herself poking Ben in the chest until her pointer finger hurt.

"I hope we can move beyond my insults. Maybe I should shower you with compliments now to make up for it." Renee rambled faster than she ever did on the radio. She took Ben's silence as permission to keep going. "I think you have a kind heart under here." She poked his shoulder and felt the muscles below his racing suit. "You showed real respect for the women on the second date last week and proved you can treat a woman right if you try." Renee paused. Perhaps she wasn't complimenting the correct attributes. Men were physical creatures who appreciated beauty, right?

"And your eyes are more incredible than anything I've ever seen." Renee took a step closer to Ben and laid her hand flat on his chest. She didn't mean to invade the space between them entirely.

She just needed to be closer to him. "It's not their color really." His breath warmed her face as she took another step forward. "It's more the way they see me…or through me, I should say. It's like they…"

All the air rushed out of Renee as Ben placed his hand over hers and curled his fingers around her wrist. Before she finished her comment, thoughts in her mind completely disappeared as her voice was silenced with Ben's lips upon hers.

Renee was so surprised she forgot to close her eyes. She even glanced at the camera to see if the person operating it could explain what was happening. She didn't know what to do. One second she was apologizing profusely, and the next, she was wrapped in Ben's arms, kissing him.

As Renee began to enjoy the softness of his lips and the security of his embrace, she quickly decided to stop analyzing everything and go with the flow. She pulled her hand from beneath his and wrapped it around his neck, placing her fingers in his dark hair and toying with its soft texture.

Just when Renee began to enjoy every aspect of the kiss, Ben pulled back.

"Finally," he said with a small smile as he placed his forehead on hers.

"Finally what?"

"You stopped talking."

Renee's face flushed. She poured her heart out to him, and he kissed her to get her to pipe down? The rush of the moment fell to the bottom of her feet as she jerked her head away from his.

"I'll have you know people all over this city enjoy listening to me talk."

Ben chuckled, grabbing her hand. "You're doing it again." He pulled her back toward him and put his hands on her waist.

"What?" She fought him off.

"Jumping to conclusions," he said into her ear. "You think I kissed you to get you to stop talking, right?"

Renee didn't say anything. For once, she was going to give him the silence he wanted.

"I kissed you to tell you I accept your apology. And because I wanted to." Ben whispered the last part so the camera wouldn't pick it up.

Renee found herself speechless.

"I'm used to it. People judge me all the time. And I've certainly given them plenty of reason to do so." Ben shrugged. "But I appreciate you saying you plan to let my true colors shine through before you reach any final conclusions. And, Renee," he said, pulling her closer, "I meant what I said the first time we met. I'm no firefighter. There's something between us, and I'm not going to do anything at all to put it out."

Renee wanted to stay in his arms for the rest of the date, but the other women waited, and she didn't want to be unfair. Plus, she was a little uncomfortable with the way she felt. She enjoyed the kiss. That much was certain. And Ben accepted her apology, which was also important to her. But why were her knees weak, and why couldn't she form any words? No man had ever had that effect on her, and she wasn't sure she liked it. She still needed to learn more about Ben McConnell before she made any final decisions. But she was sure of one thing.

He was right about the fire.

# CHAPTER FIFTEEN

RENEE HAD A hard time meeting Eva's eyes when she and Ben returned to the rest of the group. She wasn't ashamed of kissing Ben, but she didn't really want others to know. She was afraid her face revealed the truth. She needed space to sort through her emotions before the whole world saw what happened between them. Renee knew she didn't have much time since the show aired in a few days, but she would take any privacy she could get.

"Thanks for your patience, ladies." Ben took his place back in front of the expectant women as Renee sidled up by Eva on the end. "Unless anyone else has anything to say, let's get this show on the road. And let me assure you, I'll chat with everyone individually later."

Renee watched Ben place his beautiful brown eyes on each woman. When he got to her, she shuddered. Their moment together had been short, but she wasn't sure what she would do with more time. For now, she had to put the kiss out of her mind completely and concentrate on showing Ben...and the TV audience...more of her personality. Whatever might happen with Ben was great, but she needed to make sure she kept her eye on the other prize—her job on the morning show. If she accomplished both, life would be grand. If only one of the two came to fruition, at least she still had something.

Ben nodded when none of the contestants stepped forward. "And now, ladies...start your engines," Ben teased. "Today we're going to take these small race cars around the track. The stadium manager has warned me that we are not to go over fifty miles per hour. I understand that sounds slow for a racetrack, but with the curves, it'll seem really fast. The winner of the laps will get to ride in a real race car at top speed with none other than NASCAR legend Robby Labrian." Ben put his helmet on his head and opened the flap in front of his face. "Are you ready?" he asked.

Renee shuffled the dirt on the track beneath her feet and surveyed the shoes the other women wore. None were comfortable walking foot ware, much less racing shoes.

"Ready!" Eva shouted beside her as she kicked off her shoes and left them by the side of the track.

Renee smiled and glanced at Ben in time to catch his smile too. She and Ben were getting closer, but Eva was definitely going to be competition. Not only was she a nice girl, but she was beautiful, down to earth and enjoyed life with the best of them.

Clara and Tracy likely didn't want to get their perfectly polished toes dirty, so they left their high heels on and gingerly walked to their chosen cars.

"Remember, ladies, fifty miles per hour." Ben ducked into his car.

Renee removed the helmet from the seat of the yellow race car and placed it on her head. As she climbed through the window, she wondered how the other women enjoyed messing up their perfectly coifed hair. The color of the car made it almost resemble a dandelion to her as she adjusted the seat and fastened the belt around her chest and waist. She wondered why race cars didn't have doors. Perhaps to make the driver look cool when he jumped in and out of the window.

Renee played with the small key in the ignition as Tracy attempted to climb into her car. Her attire was so tight Renee worried she might be the next victim of a wardrobe malfunction. Once Tracy was in, Renee watched Clara fold herself into her vehicle. Clara wore snug clothes as well, but Renee knew her long legs hampered her attempt more than anything.

Renee started the car and revved the engine a few times. The cars were probably old pace cars put out to pasture, but she didn't care. It felt good to be in control behind the wheel. A lot of things were spiraling out of orbit right now…her job, her emotions, the result of the show… Steering this car around the racetrack with success, even if she came in last, might heighten her sense of control about her life right now.

Renee gripped the steering wheel and kept her eyes on the road. When Mike, the producer, popped up from nowhere and waved a start flag, Renee gasped. She hadn't expected to see him. If anything, she thought they would have a bikini-clad woman for the job. Perhaps Ben sent too many of those home already for them to risk hiring another.

Before Renee got left in the dust by the rest of the cars, she floored her gas pedal and took off around the track. Her car climbed to fifty miles an hour quickly and the wheel shook as she made the first turn. Ben was right—fifty felt really fast. She wasn't sure how real drivers handled faster speeds.

After the first curve, Renee was close to two other vehicles. She turned her head back for a split second and recognized the red and green cars way behind her. Those held Clara and Tracy so the two cars near her must be Eva and Ben. She drove just ahead of Eva and Ben was slightly in front of her.

Renee swerved to the left and cut Eva off unintentionally. Eva backed off quickly, and Renee realized her brief mistake became her advantage. Eva wouldn't want to hit her, and if Renee drove erratically, she could keep Eva at bay. Renee hated to thwart her friend's attempts to pass, but she wanted the race to come down to her and Ben.

By the third turn, Renee was pushing the gas pedal down farther. She was already going fifty, but if Ben stuck to the rules and remained at fifty...and was already ahead of her...it would be impossible to catch him. The needle on the dashboard rose. Fifty-one...fifty-two...fifty-three...fifty-four...her car edged forward until she was even with Ben's.

Renee didn't understand why she couldn't overtake Ben's vehicle since she was going faster than fifty, and he wasn't supposed to. On the fourth turn, when smoke filled her windshield and blocked her vision, it became clear something was wrong with her car.

Renee took her foot off the accelerator, but realized she shouldn't step on the brake either. She would risk someone slamming into her from behind at a high speed.

She closed her eyes, trying to picture where she saw Eva last. She was certain she had been on the right. Renee jerked the wheel, hoping to steer clear of an accident as her car slowed. Then she braced herself for an impact as she waited for the vehicle to come to a stop.

Renee couldn't see a thing so she squinted through the smoke and hoped for the best. Before the car came to a complete stop, a hand grabbed her wrist through the window.

"Renee! Renee!" Ben said. "Are you okay?"

Renee's eyes flew open. How in the world did Ben get to her so fast? "I'm fine." She took her hands from the wheel as the car slowly came to a stop near the finish line.

"I saw the smoke." Ben had a panicked expression on his face. "I pulled over and chased you the rest of the way."

"Where am I?" Renee removed her helmet and allowed Ben to help her climb from the window of the car.

"At the finish line," Ben answered.

Renee blinked. She drove the car blind for a good fourth of the race. It was a miracle she hadn't hit the side rails or any of the other cars, though Tracy and Clara were just rolling in.

"Where's Eva?" Renee asked.

"There." Ben pointed to grassy area in the middle of the track. Apparently, Renee's crazy driving had done more than distract Eva from passing…it had derailed her completely. "And she's fine."

Renee could tell. Eva was out of her car and heading for them on foot.

"Lockhart!" a voice yelled from the alcove in the stadium where she and Ben spoke earlier. "Lockhart!"

Renee whirled around to the sound of her name, and Mike the producer charged toward them.

"Lockhart, you went more than fifty miles an hour!" Mike yelled, his face as red as one of the race cars. "You were not to go over fifty."

"You cheated." Ben looked more amused than angry.

"How else was I supposed to catch you?" Renee asked, her knees becoming weak again. The experience was behind her, and it happened fast, but she still shook. Renee coughed. Perhaps she breathed in too much smoke. She took one small step before her legs buckled beneath her.

Ben moved faster than the fifty miles an hour car and caught Renee before she landed on the dirt track. "Oh, Renee." Ben shook his head. "Don't you know I'm the one who is supposed to catch you?"

# *CHAPTER SIXTEEN*

BEN COULDN'T BELIEVE how wonderful it was to have Renee in his arms. He needed to protect her, and he was glad he caught her when she fell. Somehow, he managed to keep a cool head. He was worried sick over her and wanted to ensure she was okay, but once he had her in his grasp, he knew she would be all right. Everything was fine. Ben didn't understand what it was about her, but whenever they were close, it was the two of them against the world. If they remained that way for the foreseeable future, nothing would stand between them.

Of course, three other women remained in the picture, and Ben hadn't ruled any of them out completely. If anything, he used his rising affections for Renee as reason to pay extra attention to the other contestants. He didn't want to overlook anyone because of the way he reacted when Renee was in his arms. He was attracted to her, he was certain of that much. But instant chemistry should not overtake what he might be able to build with the other participants.

A relationship possibility with Eva, for example, one of the most beautiful women he had ever seen. She could easily go up on a billboard and stay for all those passing to admire. But Eva had much more than outer beauty. She was also full of personality and had a heart of gold. Ben's only question regarding Eva was why she hadn't been snapped up already.

Clara, on the other hand, was a close second to Eva in the looks department. But Clara had an over-the-top beauty that started with her legs and ended with her flaxen hair. She was the type of girl displayed on the cover of a biker magazine to help showcase the two wheel rides. Ben also believed Clara had more to offer than her looks. She was gorgeous and she knew it, but Ben didn't think she was on the show to pursue his money. He understood his fortune was a bonus in her book, but she didn't seem shallow enough to go after a man for wealth alone. Ben could be wrong...he had been before. But since he had questions about her, it wouldn't be fair to count Clara out yet.

And then there was Tracy with all her red, curly hair. She had a fire in her unlike any other woman Ben had ever met. Though she seemed interested in what Ben could do for her, he got the vibe that she would be willing to reciprocate. She wasn't selfish and a relationship with her would never be one-sided. Ben liked that.

Each woman piqued Ben's curiosity. Though Renee kept distracting him with her antics, he wanted to give everyone remaining a full chance. If he was going to choose a woman on TV in front of the whole city, he needed to be sure about his choice. He didn't want to end up single again a short month after the show concluded. He would be a laughing stock. No, Ben should proceed with care. He could just as easily let his automatic attraction to Renee take over as he could Eva's stunning beauty. As long as he kept all of the women at a distance, he would be able to put perspective into the situation. He had confidence that everything would turn out okay in the end. Given time, he could make the right choice.

RENEE WANTED TO run away and hide. Her low blood pressure had taken control of the date. When she got out of the car, she shook and telltale floating bubbles appeared before her eyes. Her history told her she needed to stop and grab a hold of something, but she hadn't. Instead, Ben had to scoop her up to prevent her from meeting the ground up close and personal. Renee was embarrassed about her latest failing, but at the same time, worse happened throughout the taping process.

Once the standby healthcare team checked her over and deemed her near-faint a fluke, the taping resumed. As Renee got checked out, she got an earful from Mike.

"Over fifty…we told you not to go over fifty. These cars have seen their best days. They weren't meant for high speed."

"Thanks for your concern for my safety." Renee tried to sound sincere instead of sarcastic, though it seemed as though Mike was more concerned about possible damage to the car than her.

"The drama will be good for the show," he stated, almost to himself. "We're here to make good TV." He took a deep breath and released it.

The show had to have huge insurance to allow them to take part in a racing date. What would they have done if anyone were injured? The show would be held accountable, and any expenses that arose would have been on them. Though Renee broke the rules she also understood Mike's concerns. Just when she and Mike started to get along, she seemed to get back on his bad side. He would be bending Ben's ear later regarding Renee.

"Ladies," Ben called out to them once they stood in their line formation yet again. "What a close race." Ben spoke in a kind manner, though everyone recognized his statement wasn't exactly true. "I declare Renee the winner. Renee?" Ben turned to her and extended his hand. "I want to introduce you to Robby Labrian." Ben turned away from the group and watched the famous NASCAR driver approach from the stands.

As Robby got closer, a small squeal followed by a gasp of excitement came from Renee's immediate left. Clara rocked back and forth on her heels, and Renee wondered if she was excited or stuck in the dirt and trying to get out. One glance told her both were true. Clara threw her hands over her mouth as her eyes got wide. Renee saw her shaking with excitement.

"It's nice to meet you." Renee took a step forward as Robby approached. "As much of an honor it would be to ride the track with you..." She put her hand out to shake Robby's. "I think I've had enough of the fast-paced lifestyle today." Renee glanced at Ben. She had referenced driving the racecar, but as soon as she noticed Ben's gaze, she remembered he had taken her from zero to sixty much faster than any car ever would. "If it's okay with you, Ben, I'd like to hand my ride over to Clara."

Clara let out a small scream of delight from behind her. Renee turned as Clara rocked back and forth, attempting to extract her heel from the dirt with as much finesse as possible.

"It's your prize." Ben held up his hands. "Clara? That okay with you?"

Clara nodded wordlessly without taking her eyes off Robby.

"Okay. The rest of us will take in the action from the stands. Maybe get a chance to chat a little individually. Clara, I'll catch up with you later. Robby, go easy on the track. It's seen a lot already today."

"I heard," Robby uttered in his signature southern drawl. "Ma'am?" He held his hand out to Clara, who finally had her shoe free from the dirt.

Ben and the women stood by while Robby escorted Clara over to a car they hadn't raced earlier. He explained a few things to her about the vehicle, and she giggled at every detail. Renee rolled her eyes. Robby took over Clara's affections faster than the racecars had driven one lap around the track.

Renee followed Tracy and Eva up into the stands and took a seat on the end. Ben asked Eva to come with him, and they separated themselves. Renee fought the jealous twinge lighting up her stomach, but it was hard. She finally realized Ben was a decent guy who genuinely wanted to find love. And she might even have something with him. What his kiss did to her was unspeakable. She didn't know where things would progress from there between the two of them, but she had to admit, she wanted to be the last contestant standing in order to find out.

The car sped across the track, throwing dirt up behind every tire. She wondered how Clara's outfit fared inside. Out of the corner of her eye, she kept an eye on Ben and Eva without being obvious about her intrusion. She and Tracy stayed mostly silent, only commenting on the racetrack before them.

After a while, Ben returned and took Tracy to the same area of the stands where he and Eva had enjoyed part of the demonstration from Robby Labrian.

"I bet Clara's going nuts in there, huh?" Eva exclaimed.

"Either that or Robby is." Renee laughed. "How'd everything go with Ben?" she asked without thinking. She cared about Eva, and the last thing she wanted was for her to get hurt. She didn't want Ben to lead anyone on, including herself. If Ben was attracted to more than one woman, then she wasn't really standing out to him as she hoped.

"Well..." Eva blushed and blinked rapidly.

"That good, huh?"

"Let's just say he has very soft lips." Eva smiled.

Renee knew Eva wasn't trying to make Renee jealous, but her stomach tied in knots. "You kissed him?"

"He kissed me," Eva corrected. "And it was wonderful."

Renee sighed, trying to hide her exasperation from Eva. This was a TV show, and of course it was possible Ben would want to kiss many of the women participating. Until he kissed her, however, she hadn't cared or even really thought about it much. Once his lips met hers, though, she wanted him all to herself. She didn't want anyone else to have the experience she had.

"I guess I'm not the only one." Eva gazed past Renee to the spot where Tracy and Ben sat in the distance. Renee squinted in their direction. It was possible to be mistaken, but she was pretty sure Tracy's head was tilted slightly to the left and Ben's to the right. They were far away, but from where she sat, it looked like they were kissing.

"I can't believe him," Renee muttered.

"At least he has the guts to do it out in the open." Eva shrugged. "I mean, most men hide their cheating from you. Ben is on a TV show openly dating multiple women. What do we expect? Of course he's going to want to test the waters."

Renee stood up. She wasn't water that wanted to be tested. Like her or not...drink her down in one gulp or let her be. She started racing down the steps of the stands faster than she should have.

"Renee!" Eva called. Robby's race car began taking its final slow down lap. Renee intentionally ignored her friend, hoping she would assume Renee couldn't hear her over the race car's engine noise. Where she was headed and what she would do, she didn't know.

When she got back to the dirt track, the fast car pulled in for a stop and Robby popped out of one side. Renee froze as he gave her a swift smile before rushing to the other side of the car to gently help Clara out. She unfolded her long legs and climbed out as gracefully as possible, then looped her arm through Robby's and giggled.

"It's been nice knowing you," she said over her shoulder as she walked toward the track entrance with Robby by her side.

Renee frowned as Mike the producer chased after Clara with his clipboard. She wasn't sure she would believe it if she hadn't seen it herself. Clara was leaving the show…with Robby Labrian…the racecar driver. Renee shook her head. Love at first lap.

Robby and Clara's distraction slowed Renee long enough for Eva to catch up.

"Where were you headed?" Eva asked as she appeared at Renee's side.

"I think the question is where are they going?" Renee pointed at Clara and Robby, in a heated discussion with the producer.

Moments later, the producer slapped his clipboard against his side and stormed back in their direction. By that time, Ben and Tracy joined them. Mike whispered in Ben's ear, and the two of them took a walk down the dirt track.

Renee saw Ben's expression fall as he glanced up the path where Clara and Robby had disappeared. He shrugged, put his hands in his pockets, and returned to the other women.

"It seems Clara has left us." Ben included them all instead of just himself in the statement. "There will be no need for an elimination ceremony. Our producer Mike says we have plenty of footage from the date to get us through the broadcast, but I'd still like to spend time with you. Actually, if it's okay, I'd enjoy taking you on a real date individually. No cameras. We'll do something quiet and private. The TV people don't even have to know," he said. "They're going to tape a little more in a few minutes to explain Clara's departure and then they say we're free to go. I'll contact each of you later in the week and let you know what we'll do. Sound okay?"

Renee found herself nodding along with everyone else. Though all she really wanted to do was storm away in a fury, when Ben was close to her, with his heat permeating her skin and his cologne teasing her senses, she was powerless to do anything but agree. Though she didn't like that he kissed two other women after her, she had to hold on to what she felt when she was with him. Surely whatever he had with the others wasn't as powerful.

Renee rubbed her hands against her cheeks. Her hopes were rising too high. She needed to simmer down and step back from the situation. She hadn't come on the show to find love. She wanted to put her name out there so she could obtain her desired radio time slot, and she was doing a great job with that goal. Whether or not she had anything with Ben took the back burner. She needed to stay focused on her main goal in order to make it through this show…whether she and Ben ended up together or not.

Renee had to admit, she enjoyed the idea of her and Ben together. She didn't have to tell him…or anyone else what she was thinking. She was in for the long haul.

# CHAPTER SEVENTEEN

RENEE SPENT THE rest of the day pretending she wasn't waiting for the phone to ring. She puttered around her place, cleaning, watering half dead plants, making piles of things to get rid of and other odds and ends. She avoided going into public for fear people might recognize her and ask about the show. And, if she was being honest, she hated to think about missing Ben's call. Plus, she wanted to be alone to process all that had happened.

It had been a whirlwind of emotions. Racing faster than allowed might give an edgy quality to her personality. Those who listened to her station would not only believe her to be a sweet, bumbling personality, but also someone with a daring streak...someone who did what it took to make things happen. She thought a layered character would be better than being one-dimensional.

The idea she might be falling for Ben scared and excited her at once. Renee showed dedication to her job...and she didn't allow time to date very often. She wanted to find someone to love, but she had trouble figuring out where to meet men or how to go about finding "the one." Appearing on the show was supposed to be harmless fun and lead to career advancement. The idea that it might end up being more than that for her personal life as well as her career was unfathomable.

When Renee let herself think about the kiss she and Ben shared, goose bumps appeared on her arms. The way he held her close like she was the only one in the world made her feel more special than she ever had before. If Renee could have forced her thoughts to stay there, she would have done pretty well. But Renee never stopped there. She went on to think about how Ben might have made the other women feel when he kissed them. Eva sure seemed to enjoy her time with him. Renee wasn't sure if her emotions were real or if Ben practiced his effects on women often enough that every one of them experienced lightning bolts from his kiss.

As Renee mulled the situation over, her head spun with doubts...fears...uncertainty and everything in between. She began to clean, sort, and toss faster than before. Her frenzy almost didn't allow her to hear the phone when it finally rang.

"Hello?" she answered breathlessly on the fourth ring before the answering machine picked up.

"Renee." The voice on the other end sounded deep.

"Yes?" Renee didn't want him to think she sat around waiting for his call.

"I'd like to see you tomorrow."

"Tomorrow?" Renee paused, hoping he would assume she had to check her calendar.

"I know you don't have to go back to work until after the show airs later this week," Ben replied wisely. "And I really want to talk to you before you have to go on the radio. Maybe you'll have nicer things to say about me this time."

Renee took a deep breath. "Sure, tomorrow should be fine." She ignored the jab referring to her prior comments concerning him.

"I'll have my car pick you up at four. I want as much quiet time as possible, and it would be nice to keep things private. We don't need any pictures surfacing in the city. The TV station probably wouldn't appreciate it if they heard I took you out without the cameras, but this process is too fast, and we're all under the microscope. I need the time to get to know you."

Renee agreed. "Four will be fine," she said robotically. "Should I bring anything?"

"Nothing at all. I just want you to come over to my place. We can spend some time together. I'll cook dinner and show you what I do all day."

Renee bit her lip. He wanted her to visit his home? Completely alone? She wasn't sure she was comfortable with the idea. There were definite sparks between them, and Renee didn't want any temptations that might lead beyond a kiss. Plus, what good would the date do? She wasn't going to be able to do anything cute for the cameras to help heighten her popularity in the city. Knowing more about Ben interested her, but really, where would it lead? To a broken heart?

"Okay," she agreed quickly before she could talk herself out of it.

"I'll see you tomorrow, Renee."

"Tomorrow," she repeated and hung up the phone.

Renee collapsed in her clutter pile. She should have told him no, but how? If she wanted to stay on the show, she had to go along with his date idea. She would simply keep him at arm's length, enjoy his company, and get out as early as she could. She knew he was dangerous. The kiss they shared told her as much. She only had to survive another week or two. He would surely eliminate her. She just had to keep herself from falling for him too hard in the meantime, so she would be able to let him go as well.


BEN'S CAR ARRIVED precisely at four, and Renee was waiting. She'd been prepared for most of the afternoon, nervously pacing and trying to pretend like nerves weren't bothering her. She didn't know what to do with her hands, and she feared she might burst if she didn't tell someone. She managed to resist the urge to call to Janice, and she nearly exploded in nervous tension when the telltale long black car with tinted windows arrived.

The driver quickly exited the vehicle and opened the back door for her.

"Miss Lockhart?" he asked with a nod.

"That's me." She slipped into the car without another word.

The door closed soundly behind her as the scent of fresh leather reached her nose. The soft black seats surrounded her, and the temperature inside the car was just right. The vehicle wasn't exactly a limo, but it was definitely a luxury vehicle with all the bells and whistles. Renee saw glass separating her from the driver. She could have privacy or ask questions. She decided to leave everything untouched and try to enjoy the ride.

Renee watched the familiar scenery go by. This was her town. She knew most of the streets and neighborhoods as well as her own. She knew what building Ben lived in...everyone in the city did. It featured the biggest apartments the area had to offer. When the car arrived in front of the high rise, Renee expected it to stop, but instead, her chauffer steered toward the back and pulled into an underground parking area.

When the driver stopped the car near a bank of elevators, he hopped out and scurried to open the door for Renee.

"Sorry about this, Miss Lockhart," he said formally. "Mr. McConnell asked for discretion and wanted you to enter unnoticed."

Renee nodded. She understood. Ben didn't want anyone to know about her visit...especially those at the TV station. It was better for her to come and go unnoticed. The vehicle's tinted windows ensured no one recognized her as they drove underneath the building. And the private elevator nearby did the rest. The driver pushed the right button and released the elevator with his key. He tilted his hat as the doors closed, leaving Renee alone.

Renee fidgeted. She didn't know what to expect from the date. When she and Ben saw one another around the cameras, she used them as a shield. People were often different in public than behind closed doors. While she was anxious to see what Ben was like when they were alone, it also made her nervous. There would be no hiding...for either of them.

The elevator door opened all too soon, revealing a short hallway with lavish tiled flooring. Renee took a step that echoed up to the ceiling. She didn't wear heels, but her comfortable sandals still made a sound. Since Ben invited her to his place, Renee grabbed the opportunity to show him her true self...not that she hadn't been true to who she was before by the way she dressed. She wore nice, but comfortable Capri pants. Their soft black fabric blended in with the pattern on her light blue shirt and her sandals kept her feet happy. Renee took the casual approach to dressing and life in general. She wanted Ben to understand he wasn't getting anything fancy with her.

Renee glanced left and right. There were doors at either end of the hall. One had an exit sign above it so she assumed the other was Ben's. Ben's place must take up the entire floor of the building.

Renee was impressed by the grandeur, but she hoped Ben had more to offer than a flashy apartment.

Renee knocked softly on the door. She almost hoped Ben wouldn't come immediately, allowing a few extra moments to gather her wits. She ran her hand over her straight hair, half of which she had fashioned back with a barrette. She liked wearing her hair down, but it was long and often got in the way. She wanted it out of her face on most occasions.

Renee stared at her feet. She hoped she made the right choice for attire and reminded herself the date was mandatory if she wanted to continue on the show. The rush of air hit her from the apartment as the door opened swiftly before her.

"Welcome." Ben smiled as Renee examined his bare feet. She moved her eyes up his jean-clad legs and got stuck on his chest, which strained beneath the plain black t-shirt he wore. Shouldn't he buy a larger size?

"Hi." Renee breathed a sigh of relief. Her outfit wasn't too casual. It was far from what any of the other women would have chosen, but it suited her.

"Come on in." Ben swept his hand through the entrance. "Welcome to my humble abode."

Renee snorted as she moved into the apartment and took in the finery. The dark entry had maple wood accents and heavy marble flooring. Everywhere she looked there was an expensive item. A lavish fountain...an ornate coat rack. Renee raised her eyebrows. Ben's booming business had been good to him.

"Let's go back this way." Ben gently took her hand and tugged her away from the entrance.

Renee tried to take it all in as she flew past. The next room was a living area with pristine large white couches. They looked unused. She noticed a dining area, which might double as a conference room because of the table and chairs it featured. She wondered where the kitchen was, but didn't have time to ask. Ben led her to the back of the apartment and into a quaint space filled with computers and camera equipment.

"I really wanted to show you what I do so you could understand it…and me, a little better."

Renee bobbed her head. She desired to learn more about him and seeing his work would help. She heard some things in the news, of course. He was the mastermind behind ConArt, a photography software program that hit it big several years back. From what she knew, ConArt allowed photographers and artists to blend photos with artwork, creating a completely new piece of work. The concept became a fresh element in the art world, but average people enjoyed using the program as well.

Renee inspected the wall of work hanging behind the computers. The first picture was of a white tiger she recognized from the zoo. Ben changed the white colors to a rainbow of other colors, making the tiger appear like a fictional creature from a fantasy novel. At the same time, its real eyes stared out of the photo, grabbing her attention and reminding her the animal was not make believe.

She moved down the wall, taking in one beautiful piece of work after another. By the angles he used and the clarity the pictures held, the pieces were intriguing photos to begin with. But what Ben did with them using ConArt made them unique and unlike anything she had seen before.

"They're…beautiful." Renee struggled to find a better word to describe the work she saw. She stopped at a photo of a little girl laughing. The photo was larger than Renee's torso and the girls' pupils reflected the outline of a family.

"She's seeing her future," Ben said, close behind Renee. "Or at least her dreams for what is yet to come."

"How did you do that?" Renee was curious, but she was also trying to keep her mind off the fact that Ben stood inches away.

"I took the picture at the park. The way she looked at the ducks on the pond with such wonder fascinated me. I later drew the family outline and completed the piece using the software."

Renee nodded. Ben was an artist. He captured moments with a photograph, and he drew and blended colors to perfection. She was impressed.

"Well, everything is beautiful." She turned and bumped into his chest.

Ben grabbed her elbows and steadied her. "You're beautiful." He was inches from her face.

Renee's cheeks grew warm, and she took a step back. She couldn't let herself get caught up in the moment again. Last time she did, they shared quite a kiss and it was wonderful. But then she heard about another kiss and witnessed a third. She didn't want to be one of many. She wouldn't allow him to toy with her emotions.

Ben cleared his throat. "I'd like to create an image for you," he said. "Something unique to who you are. We can chat while I work. What do you think?"

"You mean you're going to make a custom piece I can keep?"

"A ConArt original." Ben teased. "One of a kind. I won't reproduce it, use it for any promotions or distribute it anywhere. The piece will be yours and yours alone."

"I'd really love that." Renee was touched that Ben wanted to give her a gift of that magnitude. She didn't know what he had in mind for his image, but a one of a kind ConArt creation designed by Ben McConnell would be worth a lot of money. Not that she planned to sell it.

"I'll need to take a few photos of you before I get started on the rest."

"Wait, what? Me?" She wanted a ConArt original but she had no idea he expected her to be the subject.

"Don't worry." Ben grabbed a large camera with a long zoom lens. "It'll be painless."

Renee nodded. If he wanted to take pictures of her, she needed to relax. She didn't want to come across stiff and posed in everything he did.

Ben led her to the opposite side of the room where he had a large, comfortable couch in front of a mountain scene pulled down on a screen. He yanked a few other scenes down and shook his head. "I don't think I really need much of anything," he said. "I want something to provide good light to bounce back onto your face."

"You're going to shoot up close?"

Ben nodded. "A specific part of your face."

Renee needed to show her true colors like she had for the cameras. She fidgeted. As Ben chose a background, she shook her arms and stretched her legs. He settled on a bright yellow background. When he turned around, she was massaging her cheeks with her fingers. "Just trying to warm up a bit." She gave him a cheery smile. She wasn't totally at ease with the situation, but she planned to pretend like she was until it became the truth.

"Trying singing a few scales." Ben smiled in return as he snapped several practice shots.

"Scales?"

"You know…me me me me."

"Me me." Renee sounded silly. "Me me me me." She threw her hands out, singing louder with every *me.*

"Now you're talking." Ben took pictures faster.

[114]

"Wait, are you shooting this?" Renee's embarrassment returned.

"I'm getting everything." Ben's camera snapped again. "I only need one image, but I never know when I might capture the right one." Snap. "Just be yourself."

Renee sighed and flopped onto the couch. She threw her head back onto the cushion. "Where did you come up with the idea for ConArt?" She wanted to learn as much about Ben as she possible while she had the chance.

"It was really something I did for myself," he replied as he snapped away. "I've always loved photography, and I've dabbled in painting and other areas as well. I like the way art makes me feel alive as I create it. I wanted to share that with people who enjoy it as well."

Renee shivered. She had similar experiences in her job as a radio announcer. She loved being on the air and making people laugh. She wanted to brighten their day and share herself with others.

"So you just played around with software until you got it right?" she asked.

"Something along those lines. ConArt is an idea I created many years ago and once it was discovered, it really took off. The first time anyone recognized what I was doing was when I had a tiny little art show of my own in a small store no one really knew anything about. The guy who told me it could be huge visited the gallery because of my family's legacy. Once I realized I actually had something, I took his praise seriously and built a business."

"What does your family think?"

Ben shrugged as he continued to click. "They always hoped I'd take over the family company, but they're proud, I guess. At least I succeeded, you know?"

Renee didn't have much family to speak of, but she was certain if she earned millions of dollars with an idea she concocted, all of them would burst with pride.

"So now, you run the daily operations?" She wanted to know what his day-to-day life consisted of.

"Actually, I'm more like the queen of England." Ben took the camera away from his eye.

"The queen?" Renee frowned.

"You know, sort of a figurehead. I mean, I own the company, and I have a large interest in what happens, but I've hired good people who understand the business side of things. I show up at corporate events and smile and wave for the press, but I mostly stay in the background."

Renee had a flash of Ben getting out of a limo in a tux with a stunning woman beside him. "So that's why you date so much?" she asked.

Ben laughed. "Do I date a lot?" His tone teased. "Is that what you call seeing four women at once?"

"Well, that and having a different woman on your arm for every event."

"Oh, yeah." Ben hid behind his camera and snapped more pictures as Renee waited for his response. After a long pause, Ben stopped shooting and sat down next to her on the couch. "You really want to know?"

Renee nodded.

"I wouldn't even call it dating." He sighed. "I take women out because it's expected of me. I'm an average man like any other guy who wants to find the right person to spend my life with."

"You're anything but average." Renee shuddered as Ben slid a little closer to her on the couch.

"That's not true. Sure, I have a lot of nice things and a cushy job and a company of my own, but inside," he said, reaching for her hand and placing it on his heart, "where it counts, I'm ordinary."

Renee glanced at their hands, then into Ben's eyes. His eyes captivated her. He could easily hypnotize her if she let him.

"So you're looking for the right girl." Renee tried to direct her gaze over Ben's head so his eyes wouldn't fool her. "And you date because you haven't found her."

"Right," Ben said. "I can often tell whether or not a woman is worth my time on the first date. Once I see she's not the one, I move on. Simple."

Ben released her hand, but she didn't remove it from his chest. She liked the thump of his heartbeat beneath her palm. It reminded her of the truth. No matter what the press said or even how he acted sometimes, he was a normal, everyday guy. He had blood in his veins, and a beating heart like anyone else.

"What about the women left on the show? You haven't ruled any of us out?"

Ben slid closer. "Obviously not or none of you would be here."

"And kissing each of us is your way of trying to figure it out?" she said just as Ben leaned forward, his lips searching for hers.

Ben stopped. "What are you asking?" His breath was hot on her cheek.

"Nothing, really." Renee slid her hand from his chest and stood to get away from Ben. "I'm just trying to tell you I'm not the type of girl who wants a guy who can't make up his mind. I mean, either you want me or you don't. If I'm the one for you, it should be obvious."

Ben got up and ran his hand over his hair while bracing the camera at his side. He raised the lens again and started taking pictures as Renee shifted her feet awkwardly next to the couch.

"Can you blow for me?"

"Blow?" she asked.

"Pretend like there are birthday candles in front of you and blow."

Renee gave in and blew a few times. "Are we done now?"

"I think I have all I need." Ben moved to the bank of computers to upload his work.

# CHAPTER EIGHTEEN

BEN SAT AT his computer, a look of concentration on his face. Renee wondered if the tension in the air would remain between them for the duration of the date. Maybe she shouldn't have accused him of indecision, but she didn't want to stand by and remain helpless either.

"So I know you have low blood pressure." Ben glanced at her from behind the screen. "Tell me something else about you. I want to hear a Renee Lockhart story."

A Renee Lockhart story? Now the pressure to entertain him was back on her. She could mull over her options for hours, or just jump in. In true form, she opened her mouth and began to deliver the first story that popped into her head.

"I have poor circulation too."

"Is that right?" Ben muttered around the pen in his mouth.

Renee nodded. "I got my job at the radio station in the fall and when winter rolled around, the company Christmas party came with it. This wasn't just a party with the people I worked with daily either. Some of the corporate big wigs came in to celebrate with us, and I got to meet the higher ups." Renee took a breath. This was the story she chose? Too late now. "I have a tendency to sit on my legs." She gestured down to her lap. Her legs were folded beneath her in her signature form. "The problem is that when I sit this way for any length of time, my feet fall asleep."

The clicking from the computer mouse paused, and Ben gave her a lopsided grin.

"I also like tea. And you know what happens when you drink too much tea..." Renee let her sentence trail away. She didn't want to get graphic about her need to use the bathroom when she was on a date. "Well, when I got up to use the ladies' room, I knew my feet were asleep."

"Oh, no." Ben put his hand over his mouth.

"I was used to using sleepy feet. They just have tingles in them, no big deal." Renee shrugged. "That day, my feet weren't just asleep. I swear, they were missing completely. When I put weight on the first one, it was like it was gone. I no longer had a foot. The other foot was very similar."

"No tingles?" Ben's amused expression was partially hidden behind the computer.

"No tingles. Suffice it to say I met the ground...hard and fast. The worst part of it was, absolutely everyone I worked with on a daily basis was there. In addition to the corporate head honcho and a few others pretty high up on the ladder."

"Renee."

She heard shock in his voice.

"I'm appalled."

Renee frowned. Was there something wrong with her story? Did the fact that she needed to use the restroom turn him away?

Ben stood and side stepped around the computer. "I thought I was the only one you fell for." He extended his hands out to both sides.

Renee noted his teasing tone and boyish grin.

"If I was sure that I had feet at the moment, I'd get up, come over there and smack those arms of yours back down."

Ben feigned fear and slowly lowered his arms. "You have to admit, my arms have come in pretty handy." He sat back down at the computer and started clicking again.

Renee wondered if he referred to the time he saved her from falling or when he helped her keep her dress in place. Maybe even when he put her out when she was on fire. Of course, that had been more with his entire body…

"Where do you get ideas for commercials?" Ben changed the subject.

"I hear voices in my head." Renee blurted her answer before she could think about the implications.

"What?"

Renee couldn't do anything right. She fell at his feet, lit herself on fire, pushed him into pools, told him embarrassing stories, and admitted to hearing voices. Why did he not alert security to her presence and have her escorted from the premises?

"When I have to write a commercial, I read up on the client and the information they want included. Then I close my eyes." Renee closed her eyes like she had hundreds of times before when she formed commercials. "And I hear the commercial in my head. Really all I have to do is write it down and then produce it to match what I hear."

"Interesting. Did you make the pet hospital one?"

Renee remembered how complicated that commercial had been to produce. It took a number of voice actors and myriad animal noises. "That was me."

"I know you're supposed to listen to the radio for the music, but I always looked forward to hearing that ad."

Renee smiled. She was glad he appreciated her work behind the scenes.

"What made you go into radio?"

"I got a shift on the campus station back in college," she began. "Really more for fun then anything else. When people started stopping me between classes to talk about my show, I wondered if I could make a career out of it."

"And you have."

"I have," Renee agreed. "Enough about me, I want to hear more about you. Tell me something the city doesn't already know."

"You want the dirt, huh?"

"All of it."

Renee moved her legs from beneath her on the couch and crossed her ankles on the floor. She didn't want another foot disappearing incident. Ben was clicking even faster at the computer, and she wondered how he could work and talk at the same time.

Ben spoke after a long pause. "Well, my nickname in high school was The Pits."

"That bad?"

"No, that was my nickname... *The Pits.*"

Renee frowned. She thought Ben was well-groomed. Perhaps his use of deodorant didn't come until later in his life?

"Before you jump to any conclusions, let me explain."

"Gladly."

"My parents insisted that academics were not enough. They wanted me to be involved in other activities. To make me grow up into the well-rounded person I am today." Ben grinned at Renee over the computer. "I joined the school marching band, and I didn't think I would fit in with the flutes and clarinets, and I was too lazy to carry a tuba, so I became part of the pit."

"You mean one of the people that stands on the sidelines?"

"Yes, I played the big things that couldn't be moved out on the field. Occasionally the drum set, the timpani, various standing cymbals...but mostly the mallet instruments."

"You were 'The Pits' because you were in the pit."

"That pretty much sums it up."

"And you have pictures of this?" Renee couldn't stop herself from wondering what Ben would look like in a band uniform with tassels on the shoulders and a funny looking hat.

"Only one." Ben got up from the computer and dug around on a shelf behind him. After a few moments of searching, he approached Renee and tossed a hardcover yearbook into her lap. "You find it, and I'll let you call me The Pits...but only today and never again."

"Deal." Renee resolved to scour the yearbook until she found what she was looking for. The idea of Ben in a band uniform was too juicy a prize to pass up. As she searched, she glanced up at Ben from time to time and enjoyed the look of concentration on his face. The tension between them was gone, and she grew more relaxed in his presence then ever. She was enjoying the afternoon.

After studying half the book in her lap, Renee flipped to the back and found an alphabetical page key. She found Ben's name and then had access to all of the pages he appeared on. There were only three. She searched for the first and found Ben's portrait. He had a goofy grin and a twinkle in his eye that made her think he was up to something, but he looked very similar to the Ben who sat across the room. She continued her quest and next came across a picture of the school musical. Renee squinted and held the picture close to her face. The stars of the show were in mid-dance on stage, but Ben wasn't one of them. Finally, she recognized his profile at the bottom of the stage.

"The musical?" he asked.

"That's the one."

"Yeah, I played percussion in that show. I liked to tell people that I was in every scene of the school musical. But it was only because I was standing in the orchestra pit, and my head went slightly above the stage level.

Renee smiled and wondered if Ben distracted anyone from what was going on in the musical. She wasn't sure she would be concentrating on the song and dance above him had she been there.

Her search was almost complete. There was only one page left with Ben's name tied to it. She furiously flipped to the back of the book. And there it was. A full marching band class photo. She scanned the faces until she found his. The stern look on her face took her aback. But he didn't look silly as she'd hoped. He had the marching uniform on, but the black pants and white coats with red accents were not all that bad. And instead of the hats with plumes the rest of the band wore, the percussion section had on stylish berets.

Renee sighed. "Disappointed?" Ben's voice sounded much closer than before.

"A little."

"The hat helps."

"What's up with your face?"

"What do you mean?" Ben asked in mock hurt as he threw himself on the couch next to her.

"You're so serious."

Ben imitated the stare he gave in the photo. "This is just the way I look."

Renee tried to keep a straight face, but found it impossible when met with his icy expression. She laughed until he joined her.

"It was part of being in band, especially in the percussion section. We weren't allowed to smile."

"That's not fair." Renee closed the book in her lap and raised her eyes to meet Ben's gaze. "You have a nice smile."

"Why thank you, Miss Lockhart. Yours isn't so bad either." Ben leaned forward, closing the gap between them, and Renee closed her eyes.

# CHAPTER NINETEEN

A SHRILL DING stopped Ben inches from Renee's lips. "Saved by the bell," Ben whispered.

Renee opened her eyes and swiveled away from Ben. They were having a good time together, but there were still other women involved. Her heart was dangerously close to being on the line. She needed to pull back now while she still could. "What was that?"

"My printer. Your creation is complete. But let's take a look later."

"I don't get to see it now?"

"Not yet." He waved his finger in the air. "First, we eat."

Renee followed Ben through the apartment to a small cooking space. "This isn't the main kitchen," he explained. Renee wasn't surprised. It looked like any other ordinary kitchen. "I have a staff taking care of the main kitchen...you know, for events and such. But it was awkward warming up a can of soup there, so I had this small den turned into a cooking space." Ben shrugged. "It's silly, I know, but I wanted to live comfortably in my own home."

Renee nodded. She didn't think it was silly at all, and she admired that Ben desired somewhere to call his own. She was sure the other kitchen had beauty and high quality stainless steel appliances and other finery, but this kitchen looked like a normal place to cook a meal. Ben seemed even more down to earth and human to her.

Renee backed up to the counter and jumped, placing herself in the center of the kitchen. "What can I do to help?" She attempted to see around his shoulder as he pulled a few things from the fridge.

"Not a thing. You're my guest, and I want to impress you with my culinary skills. That way, if the artwork isn't to your liking, perhaps you won't notice since your stomach and taste buds will be singing."

"My taste buds can sing?"

"Sure," Ben answered. "You know...*me me me me* like before."

Renee chuckled and found herself well entertained as Ben chopped, sliced, sautéed and scurried around the kitchen for the next half hour. When she could hardly stand the smells filling the room, he finally turned. "Dinner is served, my lady."

Ben held his hand out to her, and she jumped down. She didn't know if they would move to the formal dining room/conference room or plop down right there in the small kitchen.

"This okay?" Ben set water glasses on the miniscule table.

"Perfect." Renee smiled as she sat at one end.

Ben set a steaming plate in front of her. "Spaghetti." Renee inhaled the spicy scent before her.

"My specialty. I've been boiling noodles for as long as I can remember."

"But you did so much cutting." Renee placed the paper napkin in her lap. "I usually just pour out some sauce from a can and call it good."

Ben laughed. "Me too, but I have a special recipe for sauce, and I like to make it fresh if I have time."

Renee took a bite and closed her eyes. She would never be able to eat canned sauce again. "This is delicious," she said before swallowing.

"I'll tell my nana you enjoyed it. I used her recipe."

Renee ate faster than she should have on a date, but enjoyed the spaghetti so much she didn't want to slow down and allow it to cool. Normally, she spun noodles on her fork before eating, but with this dish, she slurped up long noodles so fast they hit her nose on the way by. After one particularly sloppy bite, Ben leaned over with his napkin and gently tapped her cheek.

"You've got a little sauce...well, everywhere." His eyes gleamed.

"Sorry." Renee raised her napkin to her lips. "I'm an enthusiastic eater. It's a good thing we're not taping today, or they'd surely do a close up of me right about now."

"That they would," Ben agreed. "One more moment to add to the montage at the end of the show."

"Montage?"

"Yeah. Don't you think they're going to put all of your tricks together into some sort of blooper reel?" he asked. "You know, the mouse dance, the fire, the race car debacle...I could go on."

"No, don't." Renee grinned along with him.

The smile slid off Ben's face. "Those are all things I love about you, Renee."

Renee frowned as she set her fork next to her plate. "You love when I push you into a pool?" She tried to lighten the serious turn the evening had taken.

"Well, maybe not so much. But the fact you had the guts to do it, yeah. You're just so...I don't know...real." Ben paused and rose as he reached for Renee's hands to help her stand. "Do you remember what you told me the first night?"

Renee nodded. She remembered every detail. She felt so smooth when she asked him to close his eyes. She planned to ask him if she sounded familiar to place herself on the radio radar before anything else.

"You actually wiped the makeup from your face...with my handkerchief. I couldn't believe it." He shook his head. Renee couldn't believe it herself. "But after that, you explained that what I would get from you was nothing but the truth. And Renee, I think you've come through. You are a genuine girl who is not afraid to be herself in any situation. You would never lead me astray." Ben paused and pulled her closer. "What I'm trying to say is that you aren't shy about being who you are. And I happen to like who you are."

Renee was speechless as Ben put his hand on the side of her face and wiped his thumb across her cheek. He drew her closer and whispered, "You had more spaghetti on your face."

Before Renee could wonder if she had bad breath from his tasty creation, Ben's lips were on hers. His kiss was light and soft, but she quickly melted. At first, her mind whirred about what he said. The idea that she was being true to her character in every situation and would never lead him astray made her stomach turn. Renee was being herself, but she was leading him down the wrong path just by being on the dating show. As he parted his lips and deepened the kiss, she could no longer think of anything.

After a few moments passed, Ben pulled back and placed his forehead on hers. "Do you want to see the creation?"

Renee managed to murmur a quick, "Yes." She followed him back to his work studio, her hand neatly tucked into his. Her heart raced inside her chest, and she didn't know if it was because of the kiss they shared or the anticipation of seeing the artwork he created using her image.

Ben sat her on the couch in the studio while he grabbed the piece from the printer and inspected it. Renee waited for what seemed like an eternity, though it was only a minute. She wanted nothing more than to be in Ben's arms again, and she wasn't sure how to address those longings. She needed to be smart about her situation, but her heart was taking over. Which should she listen to? Her head or her heart? She generally had logic and letting herself fall for Ben wasn't a particularly logical answer to her predicament. She didn't want to get hurt and she really didn't want to talk about her failure on the radio, but she would have to if she fell for Ben and got dumped.

Renee hadn't come to any conclusions when Ben returned holding a large 11x14 piece of photo paper before him backwards. All Renee saw was the white backing. "Are you ready?" he asked.

She nodded and shifted on the couch as he sat down beside her, keeping the photo close to his chest.

"I give to you"—Ben paused—"what I am going to call...*My Chosen Weed*." Ben turned the photo around.

Renee leaned forward. The image on the sheet held her lips, blowing. It must have been one of the last shots he took. In front of her lips was a bright white dandelion, which Ben had inserted with his software. There wasn't much fluff left on the dandelion and it looked like she had blown most of it away. But instead of the fluff floating away, it looked like it stuck to her lips. Renee sat back and took in the picture. She noticed flowers...or weeds in the background. A sea of dandelions. There were intricate little details she never would have thought to place into a picture. And he created the piece in a few hours. While talking to her at the same time.

"Wow." She tried to mold her thoughts into words. "You have a real talent, Ben." She reached for the picture to take a closer look. "I really think this is something I could stare at all night and still not see it all."

"You like it?" Ben bit his lip.

"Like? I love it." She wasn't sure what she would take away from the experience as a whole, but she did know this picture was something to cherish. She could look at it and remember how special she felt, even if it was the last close moment they shared. "I really don't know what to say."

"That's strange for a radio personality, right?" Ben teased.

"Very." Renee leaned back against Ben's arm on the couch and held the picture up at another angle.

Renee couldn't take her eyes from the piece. She liked the security of Ben's arm around her shoulders. The whole day had been better than she ever expected. She got to know Ben on a friendly level and she enjoyed every detail she learned about him. He was down to earth, easy going, and nothing like the media made him out to be. Sure, he dated a lot of women, but only because he hadn't found the right one yet.

When she finally put the photo down, Ben pulled her to her feet. "There's one more thing I want to do." He wrapped his arms around her waist.

"What's that?" Renee held the large photo off to one side to avoid crushing it.

"In honor of honesty, I need to tell you the truth like you promised to do for me."

Renee blushed. She had been honest about a lot of things including her personality and attitude towards life, but she still wasn't being completely truthful with Ben.

"You know the show title...*Accept This Dandelion*?"

Renee nodded.

"I got it from you."

"You what?"

"When you came in for the audition, I was there, in the control room. You said your favorite flower was the dandelion, and the idea captivated me. I asked Mike to change the title of the show."

"You changed the show name…for me?"

"Well, not really for you, but because of you." Ben squeezed her waist.

"What was it going to be?"

Ben shrugged. "Something about daisies."

"I like daisies." Renee placed one hand around Ben's neck while keeping the other at bay so the picture was safe.

"But you like dandelions better."

"True." Renee glanced over at the picture and remembered how she said something about enjoying the white fluff dandelions made and how it spread far when someone blew on the weed. Apparently, Ben remembered it too. "Hey," she said. "Did you have any part in getting me on the show?"

"In the interest of honesty, I suppose I have to answer that." He placed his lips against her cheek.

"In the interest of honesty…"

"If I remember correctly," Ben spoke softly, "I told Mike you were the one."

# CHAPTER TWENTY

BEN'S FINGER HESITATED over the phone. He needed to call the other two women, but he had trouble doing so. His date with Renee had gone well...almost too well. He smiled as he thought about her leaning against his arm as they talked late into the night. And the shock on her face when she woke up several hours later still snuggled up by his side on the couch.

More than anything, Ben remembered her soft and sweet lips on his. It was easy to admit he was attracted to her from the first moment he saw her, but now something deeper existed. He was falling for her. Hard and fast.

Ben only intended for the date to last three or four hours. He wanted to work on a ConArt project, have dinner, chat a little and wrap things up. But their talks stretched on and they simply couldn't get enough of each other's stories. They talked until their mouths were dry, and when the comfortable silence settled in and Renee's breathing evened out, Ben fought sleep. He didn't want to waste a single moment with Renee. Instead of drifting off, he gently stroked the hair from her face as she dozed.

If she had awakened and noticed him staring, she would have thought him creepy and run for the hills, but he couldn't help it. In all of the dozens of women that hung on his arm in the past, he never found anyone like Renee. Something about her made him light up. No matter what she said and did, he was always surprised, and he didn't want this experience to ever end.

When she jumped and woke in the wee hours of the morning, she gave him a sweet smile, and he relaxed his hold on her. He wanted to pick her up and carry her to bed, where he could keep her in his arms for the rest of the night and beyond. But he respected her and permitted her to set the boundaries. She allowed him one last, long kiss and asked to go home.

Ben wasn't sure how he fell for Renee so fast. It was almost like she cast a spell over him from the moment they met. He recognized her different character when she said she liked dandelions better than any other flower. He should have known he was in trouble the moment he changed the name of the show to reflect her preference.

Ben punched numbers into his phone. No more stalling. To be fair, he had to go on private dates with the other two women. No one could compare to Renee, but he promised all of the remaining contestants a little of his time off camera. His challenge would be to hide his attraction until the last show. Until that day arrived, he would go through the motions, treat the participants as friends, and let them down gently. If he hadn't already shocked the station and the audience by letting four women go on one date, perhaps he would choose Renee now and forget everyone else. But he thought he needed to honor his contract for the show and let things play out on camera.

Plus, Ben was certain Renee was the real deal…the one. If he let people watch him fall in love with her on TV, his reputation would be mended as well. Two birds…one stone. Since he didn't plan on taking Renee for granted or ever breaking up with her, the public would view him as a man of his word. He was just like everyone else. There was one right person for him, and her name was Renee.

As Ben put the phone to his ear and listened to the first ring, he couldn't believe he thought of love and Renee in the same instant. Was he falling in love with Renee?

"Hello?" a breathy voice on the other end answered.

"Hey, Tracy." He sighed. "It's Ben."


RENEE FLOATED THROUGH the next few days. She didn't want to analyze anything, but instead focused on how she felt. She still didn't like Ben seeing two other women, but she put that out of her mind and concentrated on the fact that she had officially fallen for him. She couldn't predict how things would end on *Accept this Dandelion*, but she was optimistic she and Ben would be together.

Renee viewed the show alone that week, much to Janice's dismay. She ignored the phone when it rang off the hook as she and Ben kissed in the alcove next to the racetrack and again when she blew smoke from her car and fainted into Ben's arms. She finally turned her ringer off once Ben kissed the other two women on screen. She didn't like seeing that part one bit. The scene was almost as bad as her car crash. She couldn't look away.

Instead, Renee got close to the screen. She wanted to check out the details on Ben's face as he kissed them. It was torture. When Ben pressed his lips against hers, she thought his eyes told her everything she needed to know. They were dark, passionate and glowed in the dim light of the alcove. She had seen the same expression on him the several times they kissed at his apartment. His amused look told her he wanted more of her.

As she watched him kiss Eva and then Tracy, she searched for that look. Was she headed for heartbreak? Had she fallen for a man who wanted someone else? Renee examined his expression each time and nearly convinced herself she was safe. After he and Eva kissed, he raised his eyebrows and made a slight noise. He had a happy, satisfied appearance, but he didn't seem anxious to go back for more. And when he kissed Tracy, his expression had intrigue, but once again, he didn't have that same sparkle.

Renee shook her head. She couldn't believe she sat with her nose practically pressed to the screen analyzing Ben. She didn't want to admit love for him yet. She could still get hurt. But if she wasn't mistaken, the affection may be mutual.

Renee always hoped "the one" would come to her someday. She put her career first for so long, she struggled to imagine how it would happen. There were a few radio groupies she eventually relented to dating and the occasional blind set-up, but no one she was ever serious about...until now.

And because of a local reality show, she had Ben McConnell on her hands. Of all people. She never dreamed she would fall for a man like Ben. Had he been in a line up, there's no way she would have chosen him, knowing his background. And she couldn't choose him now. The choosing was up to Ben. Until he offered her a final dandelion, Renee had to keep her desire in check. As for the radio show gig...it seemed less important. If she got the job, great. She would enjoy being on the air with Chuck in the morning show slot. If the job went to someone else, so be it. With Ben, she could enjoy love...the most important part of life.

RENEE WASN'T SURE how to approach the next radio interview with Chuck. During the past interviews, she opened up a little bit about behind the scenes items and tried to make fun of herself in order to come across friendly and approachable. She wanted listeners to appreciate her personality. The more comments that came from them, the higher the likelihood she had of getting the job as the morning show co-host across the counter from Chuck.

Being on the radio was a pipe dream Renee had from childhood on. She didn't realize it could be a real job until college, but she encountered the airwaves a few times before then. The first time she was on the radio, she was just a child. She called into a radio contest to tell the announcers about the gift she gave to her father on Father's Day. She purchased a hose nozzle because he wanted one, but once she was live on the air, she was flabbergasted and all she uttered was "nose hozzle." She knew it was wrong once it came out, but no matter how many times she tried, it came out the same.

Renee got better on the radio after studying communications in college, and her first real job went relatively well with only a few hiccups. Now, Renee had a solid job at one of the biggest stations in the area, and she was happy with her career. She enjoyed the behind the scenes script writing, and the work she did with the promotions team, but she loved connecting with listeners more than anything. Listeners often told her they felt as if they knew her when they met her in person at concerts and other station events. She made instant friends. Renee believed her passion for radio would only grow if she got on the morning show. Her career would take shape and she could start to do things for others in the community through her platform.

The grapevine, aka Janice, revealed Renee as a serious contender for the position. The station manager had a few candidates from out of the area, but since Renee already worked there and her public profile grew by the minute because of the TV show, she was a favorite. All she needed to do was finish the show.

For publicity's sake, it might be better if she got dumped on the show. She wouldn't enjoy talking about the event on the air, but she could come up with funny reasons why Ben wouldn't want to be with her...he's afraid of fire...he can't keep up with me on the dance floor...he doesn't know how to swim. Looking back at her time on the show thus far, she'd given Ben plenty of reasons not to choose her.

But Renee no longer cared whether she did what she needed to do for the sake of her radio job. Honestly, she just wanted Ben.

When she entered the studio the morning after the latest show aired, Renee longed to spill her guts on the airwaves. She wanted listeners to hear about the most incredible man she'd ever met. She wanted to admit she started the journey for the wrong reasons, but stayed because of her growing love for Ben. But she didn't know if Chuck would let her have her say. She had to play the morning by ear and see how it worked out.

"Morning, rising star." Chuck gave a swift wave of his hand.

"Right back at ya." Renee tried to keep her voice light, but her body grew heavy with anticipation. She didn't want Chuck to sense anything amiss.

The song ended through the speakers. She had cut her entrance close. "Ready to roll?" Chuck spoke too loudly as he placed his headphones over his ears.

Renee gave him a curt nod and put headphones on as well.

"100.4 KGBR. Good morning," Chuck said smoothly. "Just a couple of short weeks away from finding out who the popular Ben McConnell will pick to be his latest girl, and today we have with us our very own Renee Lockhart, one of the last three contenders in the picture. Renee, how does it feel to walk away from every show with a dandelion in your hand?"

"A little sticky, Chuck. Did you ever play with dandelions as a child? They get pretty slimy...fast."

Chuck threw his head back and laughed. "Okay, okay." He held his hands up and waved them in surrender. "I need to be more specific. Here's one you can't avoid. You kissed the guy, right? And now that you've seen last night's show, you know everyone else did too. How does that make you feel?"

Renee took a deep breath. She could discuss her emotions all day, but she didn't have to like it. She tried to avoid thoughts about the other contenders and their tender moments with Ben. But she couldn't ignore the man who she was interested in happened to be dating two other women. Renee could let her jealous side rage, but instead, she stuck to a light, comical answer. "I'm just glad I wasn't sloppy seconds...or thirds." She grinned. She wasn't relaying her affection for Ben, but she hoped to get a chance later.

Chuck laughed again and picked up his questioning where he left off. "What did you and the other girls make of Clara running off with Labrian?"

Renee whistled. "That was really something. I know the process is moving quickly, but Clara really took the fast track with Robby." Renee chuckled. "But seriously, if he can make her happy, I wish them both the best of luck."

"Is that what you're going to say to Ben if he chooses one of the other two ladies or will you be totally heartbroken?"

This was her chance. "To be honest, I don't think Ben has a choice." Now where did that come from?

"What do you mean?" Chuck tilted his head with interest.

"I've learned a lot about Ben in a short amount of time. He's not the guy everyone thinks he is, and I believe I've seen his true side." Renee didn't want to reveal too much and get Ben in trouble for their secret date. "He's a man who follows his heart. If he does what his heart tells him to, it's not a matter of choice, and I'll certainly wish him the best." Renee wanted to add that she hoped she would be able offer him congratulations in his relationship with *her* at the end of the show, but Chuck interrupted.

"Do you think he's in love?"

"I seriously hope so."

Chuck raised his eyebrows and moved on to the next song as he pulled his headphones from his ears.

"Wow." He squinted at Renee across the counter. "You're smitten, aren't you?"

Renee curled her lips into a grimace. "I am, Chuck. I really am." She wished he had asked her that when they were on the air. She longed to admit her love to the masses. It was time Renee came out of her shell to tell anyone and everyone who would listen. She had fallen for Ben McConnell, and she desired nothing more than a "happily ever after" ending to their TV love story.

# CHAPTER TWENTY-ONE

WHEN THE NEXT scheduled taping came around, Renee didn't know what to expect. She hadn't heard from Ben since their date alone at his apartment, but she also hadn't been able to stop thinking about him. She fielded several calls from Janice and finally confided her love for Ben. Janice was ecstatic, and Renee leaned toward feeling the same way. But she needed to tell Ben the whole truth regarding why she came on the show. And she still had two other women to compete against for his affections...one of which she really cared for.

As the three remaining contestants gathered in the studio in the dresses the staff requested they wear, Renee and Eva gravitated towards one another.

"Did you get to see Ben this week?" Eva asked under her breath to avoid alerting the crew.

Renee nodded. She didn't want to share too many details about her date with anyone.

"Me too," Eva said. "He rented out this whole restaurant and we had a private dinner. Just one waiter and a chef so no one else knew about it. It was really romantic being there, only the two of us. We did a little dancing after the meal even though music was nonexistent."

Renee got details she preferred not to have, but she smiled and nodded as if she wanted them.

"I had fun, though Ben seemed like he was keeping me at bay. I think he's having a hard time with this decision. He probably doesn't want to hurt any of us. But I tell you, if he chooses me in the end, I will be ecstatic. We haven't been on the show long, but I've really fallen for him."

Renee winced at Eva's words. She wasn't the only one falling for Ben. Who knew? Tracy could be in the same position as well. And if Eva fell for Ben as Renee had, she no longer had confidence regarding how Ben saw her. Renee could be in for a world of hurt. She needed to keep her hopes at a moderate level.

"How do you think Tracy's date went?" Renee searched the studio for the red-haired woman.

Eva shrugged. "She seems happy."

Renee eyed Tracy as she fluffed her bright hair with a pick. She did look happy. And as confident as ever.

Renee didn't want to think about the options for any of their futures. Seeing Ben and talking to him alone would help her think more clearly.

The producer walked in and snapped his clipboard against his hand. "Ladies. Your attention please."

Renee and Eva sauntered toward Mike and Tracy met them there.

"Today's date is a group dinner, but Ben says he really wants to speak with each of you separately too. We'll start taping and you can have a drink as a group. Then Ben can have appetizers with one of you, the main meal with another and dessert with the third. The break down might not sound fair, but you will all have equal amounts of time with him. Ben can choose who he wants for each portion of the meal. You'll ride over to the restaurant in the shuttle. Ben is waiting there. Since we have a good location for shooting the show, we'll have the elimination ceremony right there. When you aren't with Ben, you can do your on camera interviews. Does everyone understand the plan?"

The women nodded and affirmed the directions they received.

"To the shuttle." Mike waved his clipboard toward the exit.

Renee was self-conscious in her glittery blue dress. She finally borrowed something from Janice, and it wasn't her normal style. She wanted to impress Ben tonight. She needed him to like her personality, but she also wanted him to see her feminine side. She preferred hanging out in comfortable clothes, but she could dress up when she needed to. And with a man like Ben, occasions to be fancy would be plentiful.

More than anything, Renee was uneasy about being around Ben alongside two women he also had connections with. She wondered if he and Eva kissed on their private date. Eva hadn't given those details, and Renee didn't want to ask. She didn't like being in the dark about Tracy's time with Ben, but she might be better off.

The ride to the restaurant was awkward. Renee was on her way to a date that included one man, her, and two other ladies. They were close to the finale. She knew what she felt for Ben, and it sounded like Eva was on the same path. If Tracy also wanted to be the one left standing in the end, they had a serious love square.

When they arrived at the restaurant, the shuttle driver opened the door, and the ladies filed out of the vehicle. Renee saw no traffic anywhere on the street. She wondered if the TV station cordoned off the entire block for them. She followed Eva and Tracy into the restaurant. Pleasant scents of unknown seasoning and freshly baked bread met her along with the gentle lighting.

Renee spied Ben behind a raised table with drink glasses all around. She couldn't help but smile when their eyes met. Her doubts fled with one glance.

"Welcome, ladies. I hope you'll join me for a drink."

Renee grabbed a glass and eyed the candle at the center of the high table.

"Don't worry." Ben winked. "It's electric."

Renee smiled and sighed in mock relief. She didn't care to be on fire a second time. Her dress was too short to waste any material on flames. She wreaked enough havoc during tapings to last her a lifetime. Now, she needed to get down to business and tell Ben how she felt about him.

The contestants chatted with one another and with Ben as they sipped their drinks. Time ticked slowly and Renee hoped Ben would choose her for the appetizers. She wanted her time alone with him to approach sooner rather than later.

"Ben," Mike interrupted, "we need you to do an interview, and tell the cameras in what order you will be seeing each woman tonight."

"Excuse me for a moment, ladies." Ben rolled his eyes. "Duty calls."

Renee, Tracy and Eva paused their conversation as Ben walked toward the back of the restaurant. The cameras followed him, and the three women were alone. Tracy looked from Eva to Renee and then moved away to check her hair and makeup in the mirror she extracted from her purse.

"What are you hoping for?" Eva asked.

"To tell you the truth, I just want to get it over with," Renee said. "And I'm not exactly hungry."

"I understand." Eva placed her hand over her stomach. "My nerves are in high gear too. What do you think he'll want to talk about?"

"To be honest, I have something I need to say to him," Renee answered.

"What?" Eva shifted from one foot to the other.

"Well…" Renee considered her options. Ben should really be the first to hear her reasons for appearing on the show. She needed to come clean, and he deserved to know the full truth in order to make an informed final decision. But Eva was a sweet girl and telling her would be good practice. "I want to tell him about my…motives."

"Motives?"

"I didn't really come on the show to find love," Renee continued. "You might know, I'm on the radio over at 100.4 KGBR."

Eva nodded. "I listen all the time."

"Thanks." Renee accepted the compliment absent-mindedly. "There's actually an opening for a morning show host."

"Yeah, I miss Claudia."

"I want the job," Renee stated. "It's all I've ever wanted…up until now." She paused. "I came on the show hoping I could make a name for myself around the city. That way, my manager would see it was beneficial to put me in the earlier time slot."

"You want to replace Claudia?"

"Exactly. And before the show, no one considered me. My boss said I didn't have a big enough name to draw listeners. But the show has helped me out, and it's possible I'll get the job."

"Congratulations." Eva took a sip of her drink. "So, what's the issue?"

"The problem is, I'm not sure how Ben will take the news. He might think I used him. And he'd be right."

Understanding lit Eva's face. "I see. Do you have real affection for him now?"

What a strange conversation. Renee was talking about her emotions for a man with one of the other women he dated. It wasn't something that happened every day.

"I do," she answered. "I really do. I care more about Ben than any possible promotion."

Eva reached across the high table and put her hand over Renee's. "Then tell him that too. If he's the man for you, that's all that'll matter."

Tears welled up in Renee's eyes. Eva was such a sweetheart. She comforted Renee even though she hoped to have Ben herself. If Eva won his heart instead of Renee, she would truly wish them nothing but the best.


TRACY SNAPPED HER compact shut. She had a juicy little tidbit to help her wrench Ben away from the woman who he seemed taken with from the beginning.

# CHAPTER TWENTY-TWO

BEN RETURNED TO the high table as the women finished their drinks.

"I'd like to invite Eva to have appetizers with me." He extended his hand to her.

Renee smiled. She was happy Eva got to go first, but she wanted the slot for herself as well. She needed to talk to Ben, and she didn't want to put the conversation off any longer. She didn't have a choice, especially with the cameras surrounding them.

Ben led Eva to a private dining room off the main area, leaving Renee standing alone next to Tracy. She glanced at Tracy, who smoothed her hair yet again.

"Maybe I'll go do my interview now," Renee said. "In case I eat dinner with Ben. Or even if I have dessert, it'll be over and done with." She didn't know why she explained herself to Tracy. The other women raised her eyebrows at Renee as she moved away from the table to the interview area.

"Are you ready for me?"

The camera operator put a plate of hors d'oeurves aside. "Ready." He adjusted a few things on the camera as Renee stood waiting, her discomfort rising. "Okay, start by telling us what you think of this place."

"The restaurant is beautiful," Renee smiled. "I'm anxious to spend time with Ben tonight. I have some really important things to discuss with him."

"Elaborate, please?"

Renee took a deep breath. She was hesitant to say too much on camera before she spoke with Ben. She already told Eva, and Ben really deserved to be the next person to know. The cameras would take it all in. They would get their chance. And she was sure they would leave nothing out. But no one else needed to hear her confession before Ben. He deserved that much.

"I want to tell him how I'm feeling towards him, and the situation we've been in the past few weeks on the show. I haven't been as open regarding some aspects of my life, and he needs to know more about those areas before he makes any final decisions."

"Can you tell us how you feel about Ben?"

Heat infused Renee's face. Her expression probably made it obvious. She decided once she told Ben, the whole city would know. She didn't need to keep it secret. She held back the details about her possible radio gig, but she couldn't hold her emotions any longer. "I'm falling for him."

When Renee returned to the table, she found appetizers spread before them, untouched. Tracy quickly excused herself to conduct her own interview, and Renee devoured a few of the items. She couldn't name any of them, but everything tasted great. When Tracy returned, she looked from the appetizers to Renee with disdain. Renee was the only person around. She had to take the blame for eating so many of them. Her nerves got to her and with Tracy away, there wasn't anything else for her to do but dig in.

"How about those Giants, huh?" Renee tried to make small talk with Tracy.

Tracy blinked and shrugged.

"At least the weather has been nice lately." Renee made another effort.

Tracy fluffed her hair. She obviously had no interest in conversation. Renee allowed the silence to take over. After what seemed like an eternity, Ben and Eva returned. Renee thought Eva looked delighted. She glowed, but Ben appeared serious and stricken. She made a mental note to ask him about it. His relationship with Eva was none of her business, but she considered her a friend, and she didn't want her to get hurt.

"Renee." Ben extended his hand to her. "Join me for dinner?"

Renee placed her hand in his. "No problem." She should have said something more like, "My pleasure." Or even, "Of course, I'd love to." Wearing a fancy dress didn't mean she was any fancier in attitude.

Ben led Renee to the back room where he and Eva had enjoyed appetizers. The table had dandelions lying all over, and Renee wondered if the crew had to put out fresh dandelions every few minutes. The weed didn't stay decent for long based on her experience, but those on the table looked pretty nice.

Ben pulled a satin-covered chair out, and Renee gratefully sank into it.

"Why did you choose me for the dinner?" Curiosity got the best of her.

"You're the only one here who enjoys eating." Ben smiled, the sincerity sparkling in his eyes.

Renee returned his grin. She already had a plentiful amount of appetizers lining her stomach. She still wasn't hungry, but she didn't want to disappoint Ben. She would do her best to put away anything they brought out.

"Dinner is served." A waiter placed plates of fancy lobster before them.

"Thanks," Ben and Renee spoke together.

When the waiter moved away, Ben poked the lobster. "This wasn't my idea," he said. "Though I enjoy seafood, I probably would have opted for burgers and fries."

"The place on Fifth has the best ones." Renee wondered how to get into the lobster in order to eat it.

"Randy's?"

"The one and only."

"I call for delivery on a regular basis," Ben bragged.

"They deliver?"

"They do to me."

Renee chuckled and relaxed despite the stuffy atmosphere. "Okay, it's time for honesty," she said seriously as Ben's laughter faded. "I have no idea how to get into this thing."

Ben gave her a wink and reached across the table to take the lobster from her plate. He expertly cracked it in several places and pulled the meat from the shell. "It's a little strange, I know. But it's delicious. I think you'll love lobster meat. Here, try a bite." Ben dipped the lobster into the small bowl of butter that sat on his plate and leaned over the table with a sliver of meat between his fingers.

Was she supposed to take the meat from his hand and cram it in? Before she decided how to react, he had the meat against her lips. She simply opened her mouth. Her lips met his thumb as she pulled it from his fingers, and she began to chew.

"Mmm. You're right, it's delicious." Renee placed her hand in front of her mouth as she spoke. She hoped he would feed her more. She was certain the lobster tasted better because it came attached to his fingers. She wanted to be close to him like the other night. If she could have his arms around her, she would have the confidence she needed to make her confession.

This time, Renee didn't get her wish, and Ben returned the rest of the lobster to her plate. It didn't taste the same, but it was still very good after she dipped it in butter before each bite.

"You like it," Ben stated.

"I really do."

The stilted conversation stalled as they chewed.

Ben broke the silence when he cleared his throat. "I've really enjoyed getting to know you, Renee." Renee knew he referenced the other night. He couldn't be more specific because the TV crew didn't know about the extra personal time. But he was trying to get across the idea he'd had a nice time when they went on their long date alone.

"Me too." Renee shoved another bite of lobster into her mouth before she could say more. She was stalling, but the lobster was almost gone and she wouldn't have anywhere to hide soon enough.

"I hope this experience has been positive for you." The tension in the air mounted. This date was the complete opposite to the one they'd enjoyed days before. Ben acted stiff and formal and obviously talked more for the cameras. It was weird being on camera, but there was no avoiding it, and Renee needed to take advantage of every minute she had with Ben.

"It certainly hasn't been what I expected." She wiped her mouth with the soft, cloth napkin.

"How so?"

Renee scratched the palm of her hand. They were sweaty from the nerves, but they suddenly itched like crazy.

"I wanted to talk to you about that. This experience...you...everything." She wasn't being very clear, but with any luck, it would all come out in a coherent manner before their time ended.

"Nothing has been what I expected either," Ben agreed.

Renee tried to concentrate on what she needed to say, but the room suddenly became very small and hotter by the minute. She removed one shoe and scratched the bottom of her left foot against the leg of the chair while she forcefully scratched the palm of her other hand.

"There's something you need to know, Ben." Renee tried to get her shoe back on before anyone noticed, but instead she kicked the right shoe off and started scratching that foot on the table leg as well.

"What?" Ben leaned across the table. "You can tell me anything."

Renee tried to form the explanation. She had them in the back of her throat, ready to spill out. At first, she thought the stuck words were the reason she was having trouble breathing. But when breaths became even harder to take, she forgot all about her planned admission.

"I...I can't breathe." She threw her hands around her neck and stood from the table.

"Renee." Ben shouted and rushed to her side. "You're swelling up!"

The last thing Renee remembered were Ben's strong arms scooping her up. She thought she heard Eva gasp as they flew by. When she woke up later, she was in a hospital bed with beeping and whirring machines around her.

BEN HAD BEEN petrified by the expression on Renee's face when she realized she couldn't breathe. He had never been more scared in his life. He rushed her out to the shuttle car, which luckily still sat out front and fled to the hospital.

It didn't take more than a few minutes for the doctors to figure out Renee must be allergic to lobster. Her hands and feet were red from her scratching and her throat was swollen nearly all the way shut. Had they arrived much later, she may have been in serious trouble. They administered a shot and put her on an IV for fluids. She would be fine.

Mike wanted Ben to return to the restaurant to finish taping, and Ben assured him he would, but not until he knew Renee was okay. When her eyes fluttered open, Ben took hold of her hand.

"I'm so sorry." He squeezed her still swollen fingers.

"What happened?" Renee asked in a weak voice.

"Apparently you're allergic to lobster." Ben gave her a sheepish smile.

"Does this mean I don't get to have it again?"

Ben chuckled. "I think that would be best."

"But it was so delicious," Renee complained.

Ben laughed. He stroked the hair away from her face with his free hand.

Ben glanced at the camera over his shoulder. "I'm sorry. I wouldn't have allowed the camera in here, but they insisted when I told them what I planned to do."

"What do you want to do?" Renee whispered.

Ben pulled a squished dandelion from his jacket pocket and presented it to her. It sagged before her. "I wanted to give you this...sad as it may be." He sighed. "Renee, will you accept this dandelion?"

"Yes." Renee took the weed from his hand and placed it against her chest.

"I have to go back to the restaurant and complete the elimination ceremony, but I needed you to know that I want you to stick around."

"Is this a pity weed?" Renee asked.

"Pity weed?"

"Are you giving me this because I almost died?"

Ben chuckled. Her humor was one of the things he loved most about Renee. She had a way of finding the funny side to any situation. "No, Renee." Ben attempted to remain serious. "I'm giving you a dandelion to show you how I feel about you."

Ben watched a smile light Renee's puffy face. She would probably kill him later when she saw her appearance on TV. He was the person who allowed the cameras into the room. But for now, he enjoyed the expression on her face. To him, she was beautiful even at a larger than normal size.

"I'll check in on you again soon," Ben said. "The doctors say you'll to have to stay for a few days to allow the swelling to go down. You need extra rest, and they want to make sure you remain hydrated and don't have any further adverse reactions to the lobster. Until then, keep my dandelion close. I'll be thinking of you."

Before Renee said anything wacky to ruin the romantic moment, Ben kissed her on the forehead and left.

# CHAPTER TWENTY-THREE

RENEE WAS BORED stiff in the hospital. Janice often stopped after work, and her visits helped stave off the long hours alone. The nurses popped in every hour or two as well, usually when Renee tried to sleep. She couldn't wait to get back to her regular life...as if anything about her life was normal.

On one side, she had her radio job, which she loved. She still somewhat hoped for a promotion to be on the morning show. But she also had Ben to consider. He might be the one she'd been dreamed of finding all her life.

Renee doubted the two could coincide once Ben found out why she came on the show in the first place. She still needed to tell him, but the world worked against her. Every time she tried to explain, something happened to stop her. The last time she almost died. She wondered if a force greater than her was conspiring against her to keep her secret. Maybe Ben didn't need to know.

Ben called a few times, and the nurses commented on the glow Renee had on her face afterward. He never said much, just that he anxious to see her again. He often apologized profusely for serving her lobster as well.

Renee was tempted to ask him how the rest of the taping went, but she didn't want to bring up anything show-related. She enjoyed the sound of his voice and pictured the way he looked into her eyes. She knew the producer insisted Ben return to the restaurant and finish recording. The elimination ceremony continued without her, though she already received a dandelion. She didn't know who he eliminated, and it drove her crazy. Unless she worked up the nerve to ask him directly, she had to wait until the show aired to find out.

Renee asked the nurses not to disturb her during the episode if possible. When the theme song began, and the announcer started spouting off his usual cheesy lines, Renee groaned when her door opened. Either there had been a shift change and someone hadn't gotten the message or the nurses were disregarding her request. She hit the mute button on the TV to take care of whomever it was fast and get back to watching.

An instant smile widened her mouth as her eyes met Ben's piercing brown stare.

"Ben." She tried to cover her legs with the sheet and hide the thin hospital gown she wore.

"I hope I'm not imposing. I didn't want you to see the show alone."

Renee beamed. She looked like hell after three days in bed, but she couldn't have been happier to welcome him. "My friend Janice would have come, but she had to work a concert tonight."

"I'm glad I was free," Ben said in his familiar teasing tone.

"Is this okay?" Renee asked. The producers didn't want any of the participants seeing one another outside of the tapings. That way, they would capture anything and everything they needed on camera.

"It's okay with me if you agree. I couldn't care less what anyone else thinks."

"It's definitely fine with me." Renee glanced over at the TV. The date started, but seeing Ben was more important.

"May I?" He waved his hand toward the side of her bed.

Renee scooted over, and Ben sat beside her, leaning onto the pillow she had shoved behind her back. Renee's temperature rose with his body pressed against her side. She reached for the control on the side of the bed and un-muted the TV. Ben grabbed for her hand, lacing his fingers through hers. It would be hard to concentrate on the show with his presence, but she had to try.

Renee leaned against Ben's arm and enjoyed his fingers between hers as he greeted the women on camera and asked Eva to have appetizers with him. Their conversation flowed well, and Renee marveled at Eva's calm, cool, collected manners. She was a wonderful woman, and any man would be lucky to have her. Eva reached for Ben's hand across the table, and Ben didn't pull away. He also allowed her to kiss him on the cheek before they returned to the others, but that was as far as they got. Their time together appeared to be between two good friends.

Watching Eva with Ben made Renee sad. She saw Ben wasn't as into Eva as Eva was Ben. But based on how Eva acted when she got back to the table, she must not grasp that idea.

Before the commercial, they showed Eva's interview, and she gushed about what a wonderful man Ben was. She even said she would be over the moon if he picked her in the end. Renee flinched when Eva admitted she was falling head over heels for him and planned to commit herself to him if he chose her.

Renee glanced over at Ben, who worked his jaw back and forth. He was seeing the interviews for the first time, and she wondered what he thought. It was enough to have him there experiencing it with her. She didn't want to overanalyze anything.

After the commercials ran, the show came back on, and Ben extended his hand to Renee and invited her to the main course of the evening. Renee watched as she scratched her palms on camera. Luckily, they hadn't caught her rubbing her feet against the table and chair legs. She noticed the swelling running up her neck and into her face. It happened so quickly she only imagined what Ben thought.

"I thought you were nervous," Ben supplied. "You said you had something to talk to me about, and your face got all red. Seeing it on camera, I can definitely tell you were swelling up...fast."

"The camera adds 10 pounds, you know." Renee squeezed his hand as he chuckled.

On screen, Ben rushed Renee out of the restaurant. The announcer took over and explained Renee's allergic reaction and included that she was hospitalized, but recovering nicely. Then, they showed Renee's interview in which she admitted to her attraction to Ben. Renee felt Ben press his shoulder harder against hers. She wished they were alone and not stuck in a hospital room where a nurse could barge in any second.

After her comments, they cut to a confession from Ben. "I was so worried about Renee," he said. "I didn't want to leave her side at the hospital, but you know what they say...the show must go on. I convinced the nurses to allow me to take a couple of cameras in with me when I visited Renee, because I needed to do something before I left her to recover."

Renee smiled as Ben gave her a dandelion on screen. Tears welled up in her eyes at his words. She wasn't sure if she should cover the screen out of horrification due to her swollen face or be amazed that he still gazed at her with such gentle appreciation.

Overall, she was glad he came back in to give her the dandelion. She had it pressed in the hospital information guidebook next to her bed.

When the show paused for another commercial break, Ben turned toward Renee and put his hand on the side of her face. "I can't wait until this is over." He placed his forehead against hers. "There's only one more taping session."

Though he didn't say anything specific, his eyes promised her a future.

"Me too," she whispered, closing her eyes.

Ben leaned forward slightly and brushed his lips against hers. When he pulled back, Renee wanted nothing more than to lean in and capture his kiss again, but the program returned, and she wanted to see his time with Tracy and the elimination ceremony.

On screen, Ben returned to the restaurant and informed a worried Eva and a bored Tracy what happened with Renee. He invited Tracy to the private room for dessert. This portion of the date was even harder to view than the appetizer section when Ben ate with Eva. Renee didn't want to be jealous of Tracy, but she was more bold and flirtatious than Eva. She made enough comments to allow anyone to know what Ben would get from her if he chose her. Renee shifted on the bed. Ben was her boyfriend, or so she wished, and she didn't enjoy hearing another woman speak to him that way. Even worse...he seemed to be going along with it. She suspected he only feigned interest for the cameras, but how could she know for sure?

Renee wanted to take her hand out of Ben's. She didn't like being close to him while Tracy fawned over him. But as she tried to pull away, he held her fingers tighter. They remained silent as the elimination portion of the evening came on and the dramatic announcer told viewers Ben only had one more dandelion to give since he gave one away to Renee already.

Ben stood before the two ladies and held up the one remaining dandelion. "I want to thank both of you for going through this journey with me. I've enjoyed learning more about you, and I know there's a wonderful man out there for the woman I'm not asking to stay. With that being said, Tracy?" Ben paused and waited for her to approach and stand in front of him. "Tracy, will you accept this dandelion?"

Tracy threw her arms around his neck and pressed herself against him, including her lips on his. "Of course," she said breathily as she pulled away.

Ben shook his head and extended his hand to Eva. "Can I walk you out?"

Eva nodded, and he escorted her to the shuttle outside the restaurant. "I'm sorry, Eva. You didn't do or say anything wrong. You're a wonderful woman, and you deserve love more than anyone."

"Thanks." Eva's lip quivered. Renee wondered what she would say in Eva's position.

Based on the tears in her eyes, Eva was hurt, and she didn't want to let Ben go, but there wasn't an option. He made the decisions.

The show hit another commercial break, and Ben turned to Renee. "I wanted to be with you when you saw that."

Renee squinted at him, unsure as to why.

"Eva is a wonderful lady," he continued. "You two hit it off and formed a friendship during the tapings."

"We did," Renee affirmed.

"I let her go because I saw she invested her emotions in the process. She was...interested in me...and I didn't want to hurt her any more than I already did. Leading her on just wasn't right. As soon as I made my decision, I wanted to send her home. She deserved better."

Renee nodded, speechless. Did Ben say he made up his mind? The fact that he watched the show with her caused her hopes to soar. "She's a fantastic person."

"She is, and I hope she finds someone to love. I would have been lucky to have her, but she wasn't the one for me, you know?"

Renee understood. She still felt sorry for Eva, her friend. She was beautiful, full of personality, and down to earth to boot. She deserved a partner in life, and Renee sincerely hoped she found him soon.

The TV drew their attention as the announcer profiled the two remaining contestants. "Who will Ben choose?" he said. "Renee...or Tracy?" As the announcer talked about qualities each woman held, the screen flipped through photos and videos of them from the show tapings. Tracy's shots included her in a bikini, her tight dresses and high-heels, and her flaming hair shining perfectly. Renee's were more unique. They showed her in flames, her dancing like a mouse was attacking, her pushing Ben into the pool and so on.

"Wow," Renee said as the credits ran. "I think I know who I'd pick." She laughed. The show made Renee look like a complete disaster, but based on the material she gave them, they had no choice.

"So do I." Ben turned to Renee again and placed his thumb beneath her chin to raise her eyes to his. "So do I."

# CHAPTER TWENTY-FOUR

RENEE RECEIVED HER discharge papers and left the hospital with a spring in her step. And it wasn't because the swelling disappeared. She was well rested and had a clean bill of health.

"Being admitted did you good." Janice opened her car door for Renee.

"You make it sound like I got forced into the mental ward."

"I can think of worse places for you to land." Janice slid behind the driver's seat.

"Like where?"

"Anywhere...with a broken heart."

"Well, I feel great." Renee ignored Janice's pointed stare.

"After the train wreck of a show, I'm glad." Janice laughed. Though she worked the concert during airing, she recorded the program and devoured every second when she got home. "I never would have suggested you audition had I know you'd end up in the hospital puffed up like a blow fish."

"That bad?"

Janice puffed out her cheeks. "That bad. I can't believe he gave you a dandelion with your face twice its normal size. That boy must really be interested in you to overlook your balloon impression."

"Come on now," Renee scolded as they pulled away from the hospital. "Some men like balloons."

Janice crossed her eyes and clicked her tongue. "What's planned for this week?" She always dug for more details.

"I'm not sure," Renee answered. "Something tells me romance will be in the air." She raised her eyebrows at Janice. "How did Chuck do on the show?" She regretted missing the morning after interview. She wanted to call in and go on the air over the phone, but the nurses insisted she rest, and Chuck was on the air during hospital quiet hours. Since Renee stayed up late in a daze over Ben's sudden appearance, she slept right through the radio program and didn't even listen.

Janice shrugged. "He did okay. You know Chuck. He always has something to say."

"And what did he say about me?" Renee could handle it. She had a thick skin.

"It wasn't you, really. But more Ben."

"Oh?"

"Chuck thought he had interesting taste in women. A flaming redhead and a flamer."

"Ah, of course, going back to the fire again. Is anyone ever going to let that go?" Renee asked.

"Not likely, girl. Not in your lifetime."

Renee didn't reveal anything about her secret visitor. Hospital personnel saw him, but since he came in the back entrance, and Renee already asked not to be disturbed, not many people knew about their time together. And so far, the word hadn't leaked to the public. Though Renee and Janice were close, she wanted her friend to see the finale on live TV. She wouldn't ruin the mystery for her. And while she was fairly certain what the outcome would be, she didn't want to get over confident. After all, Ben hadn't directly told her he would choose her.

Renee let Janice drive her home, and her friend caught her up on station gossip that didn't revolve around her. Once she settled in on her own couch, Janice left and promised to bring lasagna over later. Renee was perfectly capable of handling meals on her own, but Janice was a good friend, and she appreciated her help.

Renee had a couple of days to prepare for the finale. She had one more date with Ben...as would Tracy. After those dates, they would meet once again for the final elimination ceremony. This time, Ben would speak to them separately. One of them would leave empty-handed while the other would receive the last dandelion.

All Renee could do was wait, dream, and hope. Whether or not she got a higher position at the radio station, she felt certain she had wedged herself into Ben's heart...where she was meant to be.


BEN SLIPPED ON his button down shirt. It was the day of his last date with Renee before the final dandelion ceremony, and he wanted everything to go well. He told the producers he planned to choose the date on his own. He wore casual attire and asked for handheld cameras. It was time to get away from the finery and enjoy the day with Renee. He chose an activity he thought would bring her personality out and allow her to shine. She captured the viewers' hearts with her mishaps and somewhere along the way, she had grabbed his as well. Now, everyone would see exactly why he loved her.

He would take Tracy on the date the producers planned. It was another fancy dinner and some dancing, complete with a local celebrity band for a final surprise. He didn't want to bother with the date, but he had to go through the motions. He was glad Tracy was left instead of Eva. Eva didn't deserve to be led on. Ben had hopes for Tracy in the beginning, but the more he learned about her, the more her true colors showed. She tried too hard for his tastes, and she obviously wanted something from him other than love and affection. She would make some man happy, but not him. He didn't like leading Tracy on either, but based on his opinion of her, it was better to hurt her than sweet, considerate Eva.

Not much longer, and he could finally tell Renee exactly how he felt about her. She must have an inkling already, but saying the words and seeing the realization spread over her features would be priceless. Her face was so expressive. He couldn't wait to see it light up when he told her she was the one he wanted to be with. There was no one else.

# CHAPTER TWENTY-FIVE

RENEE COULDN'T HAVE been more excited for her last date with Ben. In the hospital, he told her it would be a "come as you are" outing. It sounded like her kind of activity. Jeans were the way to go. Granted, she put on her best pair of jeans, but still.

Renee arrived at the studio filled with anticipation. The TV crew whirred around the set, getting ready for the finale which would take place in a few days. Renee couldn't tell what changes they were making, but the end was near, and she got goose bumps at the thought. She imagined standing before Ben, all dressed up again with hope in her eyes. Once he told her how he felt and offered her the last dandelion, their life together could start...away from the microscope and the TV cameras.

"Renee," Mike barked with his ever-present clipboard in hand. "Shuttle's here."

Renee nodded and headed for the exit. She hoped Ben would pick her up so they could spend even more time together, but she couldn't complain. She got him to herself for the whole day...except when he had to step away for TV interviews...and despite the fact that they would not be alone with cameras recording them continually.

When the van pulled up to the city zoo a few moments later, Renee wondered if they had taken a wrong turn and pulled over to get their bearings. Ben told her to dress casually, but the TV station would never plan this as a date. It was so normal and everyday...and Renee loved the idea.

As the shuttle came to a full stop at the front entrance, Renee squealed. Ben stood inside the gates waiting for her. Even from a distance his tan skin glowed. She stared as he ran a hand through his hair. She couldn't wait to get closer, and see the joy on her face reflected in his eyes.

Renee jumped out of the van and jogged under the entrance arch. Several people milled about, and when they noticed Renee, Ben, and the cameras, they pointed and stared. Renee didn't care. She threw herself into Ben's arms, and he twirled her in the air.

"Feeling better I see?"

"Much." The puffiness all around her face went away at the hospital, and the red bumps on her hands and feet completely disappeared a few days later. Though the incident was scary, she now recognized her allergy and would not eat shellfish again. Especially on TV.

"I thought we'd enjoy some time outside and see some animals."

"That sounds great," Renee said enthusiastically, still in Ben's arms.

"Where do you want to go first?"

"Aquarium."

"To the aquarium." Ben loosened his grip on her waist and laced his fingers through hers.

"I can't believe our last date gets to be so...normal."

[167]

"Actually, coming to the zoo was my idea. Since it happened last minute, they weren't able to clear the whole zoo for a private viewing. But the onsite personnel ensured that we would be able to move forward without too much interference. We have the whole day, and they can edit out any interruptions."

Renee wrapped her free hand around Ben's arm. She loved the idea that he planned the date with her in mind. The day would be casual and easy going, and it lined up with her personality exactly.

Once they entered the aquarium, they stepped into another world. It was dark, but a bright blue wall lit up the space before them as silver fish swam in circles.

"I wonder if they ever get tired," Renee pondered out loud.

"Depends," Ben said as Renee tore her eyes from the fish and caught him staring at her. "On whether or not they truly love it."

Renee narrowed her eyes.

"If swimming in circles is what they really love, they probably never get tired of it. They might even look forward to it. In fact, there's likely nothing that can keep them from their circles."

"Good point." Renee wondered if Ben still talked about the fish.

They moved through the aquarium at their own pace, ignoring the cameras following them as much as possible. Near the end they reached a large tunnel that placed them in the aquarium. With water surrounding them above the thick glass and fish, sharks and turtles swimming beside and above them, it was like they were in the ocean.

"People get married here," Ben said quietly as he encircled Renee's waist with his arm.

Renee drew in a deep breath. "Where do they put the guests?" She tried to keep the mood light. "In with the sharks?" The display was long and narrow, but there wasn't much room for seating.

Ben chuckled. "I should have guessed that's what you'd say."

Next Renee wanted to visit the lions and bears, but she didn't mind the walk between the displays. With Ben's warm hand pressed against hers, she felt complete.

"The lions are so majestic, aren't they?" she asked as a lioness stared at them without blinking.

"They definitely seem to know what they want."

"I think they want us…for lunch."

"Oh, come on. You'd just be a little snack." Ben tickled her side.

When they arrived at the polar bear display, Renee was fascinated. The large bear dove into the water and began swimming laps in his pool. The way he swam one direction, turned and paddled back had her transfixed. The bear was content, and she was as well.

When the polar bear finally climbed out of his pool and shook himself off, Ben turned to Renee. "Monkeys?"

"Monkeys," Renee affirmed. She was enjoying the day more than she imagined when they first pulled up. She and Ben were flirting more. They were always physically connected at the hand, but they kept things light for the cameras. There were a lot of things they needed to talk through, but those items were between the two of them and no one else's business.

Since her hospital stay, Renee decided to back off on telling Ben why she auditioned for the show and agreed to be one of the bachelorettes vying for his affection. She still wanted him to know, but she planned to tell him after he chose her. She didn't want to ruin the magic the show created. The issue was something they would have to deal with in the real world, but everyone in the city didn't need to know.

She would tell Ben. For sure…after he made his choice.

When they arrived at the monkeys, Renee let go of Ben's hand and raced over to the waist-high bar near their cages.

"Oh, what fun," she said as they swung from branch to branch. The monkeys played and raced through the trees within their enclosure. "A baby." She pointed to a mama monkey swinging around with a baby clinging to her neck. "It looks like she's going to fall off."

"She'll hang on if she knows what's good for her." Ben gazed at Renee.

"Oh, I think she knows." Renee winked.

They enjoyed the monkeys for a few more moments but when they turned away, Renee observed a red streak rush by her out of the corner of her eye. She glanced down in time to notice a toddler swing under the bar. The little girl put her fingers through the monkey's cage and gazed up at them with wonder.

Renee looked over her shoulder, trying to place the girl with a parent of some sort. No one was around.

"Ahhh!" the little girl screamed as a monkey reached its paw out of the enclosure, grabbed her bright red shirt and pulled her against the cage.

Renee swung herself under the bar. She grasped the monkey's paw and tried to pry his fingers from the girl's clothing.

"It's okay," she said as calmly as she could. "Mr. Monkey likes your pretty shirt. Don't worry. He'll give it back."

Renee smiled at the girl, trying to convey her calm spirit as she attempted to loosen the monkey's fingers from the toddler's clothing. The girl had big, fat tears running down her face. She was nearing hysteria. Being a stranger, the girl was probably afraid of her. Plus a monkey had her shirt in his grip and wasn't showing any signs of letting go.

"Okay, Mr. Monkey," Renee addressed the primate. "Time to release our friend."

The girl wailed again.

"Let go!" Renee yelled. She tried once more to gently lift the monkey's fingers from the girl's shirt. The monkey let out a screech, and Renee jumped back. He pulled the little girl closer to the bars, sending her into a new wave of frantic crying.

"Oh no, you don't." Renee reached her hand through the bars and gave the animal a sound slap across the face.

At first the monkey stared at her, stunned. Then, as if resolved that she wasn't going to let him have his way, he released the girl, belted out another screech, and swung into the nearest tree.

Renee helped the little girl back under the bar and then ducked under after her.

"Emma!" a woman called. "Emma, there you are. Are you okay? You were crying? You can't run off from me."

Ben grabbed Renee's elbow as she stood, and the frantic mother scolded the girl for disappearing.

"Thanks for your help," the mom said over her shoulder as she escorted Emma from the monkeys.

"She has no idea what happened," Ben observed.

"Think she'll notice paw prints on her shirt later and ask?" Renee shrugged.

Ben turned to her and frowned. "Did you really just slap a monkey?"

Renee burst out giggling. "I believe I did."

"Remind me never to get on your bad side."

Renee laughed so hard tears bigger than those on the little girl's face ran down her cheeks. Ben laughed along with her. The two were in hysterics and people stopped to watch them, this time not because of the cameras.

"Did you see the look on his face?" Renee gasped.

"He was like 'oh no, you didn't,'" Ben replied.

After a long laughing spell, the two calmed down enough to move on, though they couldn't stop discussing the incident. They continued through the rest of the zoo until they found themselves out in the corner as far as from the entrance as possible. A couple of elephants lumbered around in the mud, enjoying the evening breeze.

"This has really been something." Ben's arm pressed close against Renee's as they leaned on the bar, and the large creatures sprayed each other's backs.

"It has." Renee fought back another fit of giggles as she thought about the monkey. "And I have you to thank. It was your idea."

"Well, I can't take credit for everything. There's one more surprise tonight, and I had nothing to do with it. Come on, I'll show you." He grabbed her hand and led her through the flower garden at the back of the zoo. On the other side, sat a small gazebo glittering with white lights. As they went up the few steps to the center, Renee took in the intimate table set up at the center. "Care to have a picnic?" Ben asked as he drew a basket out from under the seat in the gazebo.

"Don't mind if I do," Renee said. The day's activities made her ravenous.

Ben laid out a spread of crackers, cheese, fruit and other items. Before they dug in, the TV crew dragged Ben away for another interview. He disappeared on occasion throughout the day, and they talked to Renee several times as well. Renee resented the interruptions, but it was part of their situation and would be a thing of the past soon.

When Ben returned, Renee had a plate ready for him, and the two enjoyed watching the sunset at the back of the zoo as dusk settled in. Renee told Ben about her family, and Ben described new projects he wanted to take on with ConArt.

As the meal came to a close, a lone violin sounded from somewhere in the garden.

"What's that?" She squinted into the darkness.

"It's for us." Ben stood and extended his hand to her. He led her down the gazebo steps onto the sidewalk nearby.

Renee looked up at him as he wrapped his hand around her waist. His eyes twinkled from the reflection of the lights shimmering on the outside of the gazebo. He smiled at her, but his face remained serious. Renee put her hands behind his neck, and they began to sway to the music.

At first, neither of them said anything. Ben bent over and kissed Renee briefly before pulling back to allow a couple of inches between their faces.

"Renee, I can't wait to be as honest with you as you have been with me."

Renee blushed. Perhaps she should reconsider her choice to save the truth for later.

"It's hard for me to keep my emotions inside. They're so strong. My only comfort is that I'll be able to tell you everything soon."

Renee stood on her tiptoes and kissed Ben. Their swaying stopped as they allowed the moment to take over. Renee didn't want to reveal the depth of her feelings until Ben was able to do the same. She hoped the kiss would show him everything he needed to know.

# CHAPTER TWENTY-SIX

THE SET APPEARED completely different than during previous elimination ceremonies, and Ben wished he could enjoy it. Instead, he reeled from his date with Tracy. Everything went well with Renee, besides the monkey incident. He should have guessed she was too good to be true.

"I don't want to be the girl who spreads rumors about other contestants," Tracy said early in their date after Ben deliberately kept her at arm's length. "But there's something you should hear about Renee."

Ben almost didn't want her to continue. Tracy was the type who could concoct believable stories and bend them to make whomever listened eat them up. And if she'd been indicating any of the past contestants, he might not have cared. But when it came to Renee, he couldn't resist.

"You really should know this piece of information before making your final decision. I'm not trying to sway you in either direction," Tracy continued. "You should have all the details so you can make an informed decision."

*Yeah, right.* Ben nodded feigned appreciation. He wanted her to spit it out already so they could get the rest of the date over with.

"Renee didn't sign up for the show to find love. In fact, she almost ducked out of the tapings entirely when she learned you were the bachelor. She moved forward with the process because she hoped to get a promotion at work. She works in radio, right? And apparently she wants a better time slot or something."

Ben's heart beat hard in his chest. He tried not to show his emotions as Tracy spoke. Renee almost dropped out of the program because of him? She told him she didn't want any of her preconceived ideas of him to get in the way. Was she a better actress than she let on?

Being on the show raised her public profile, and if she desired a promotion in her radio job, the antics she'd pulled would get her name out there. People would remember the girl who caught fire over the one who stood in the background in a glittery dress. Ben wanted to believe in his love for Renee, but too many women had used him in the past. He didn't want to be a skeptic, but in his book, women were all the same. He thought Renee was different, but what Tracy told him proved him wrong.

"Thanks for the information." Ben went through the motions for the rest of the date and tried his best to appear as into Tracy as she was him. He held her close, let her kiss him, and matched her flirty tone. His heart wasn't there, but he had to put on a good show in case he decided to change his mind about the finale.

As Ben watched the final preparations for the last elimination ceremony, Mike approached from the side.

"So…what's it going to be? Or should I say who?"

Both women were set to arrive at the same time, but they would be ushered to different parts of the studio and wouldn't see one another. Ben had to tell the producers who he wanted to speak with first. The person who would be first was the one he would let down and the second candidate would be his chosen bachelorette.

"Time's ticking." Mike tapped his clipboard. "The ladies will be arriving shortly, and we need to start taping right away. There's a cooking show set to air live in the morning. We have to re-arrange the set tonight."

Ben glanced at Mike. He was trying to make the most important decision of his life, and he was being pressured because of a cooking show. He crossed his arms over his chest, bolstered by the pull of his tuxedo jacket across his back. That made him think of Renee's dress ripping during one taping and he smiled.

"Okay, okay." He held up his hands. "I know what I want to do. I know what I *have* to do."

RENEE COULDN'T BELIEVE she made it all the way to the end of the show. On the first night, she was certain she would be headed out the door. She gave Ben every reason to send her away. Well, almost every reason. She still needed to tell him about her motives for being on the show, but once he chose her and they were together, surely she would form the words in a way that wouldn't make them sound too bad.

When Renee arrived at the studio a bundle of nerves, she was confident about the outcome of the taping, but she didn't know how she would react when Ben finally told her how he felt about her.

Renee spent enough time with Ben to read certain things about him. She knew him enough to understand what his eyes said without hearing any words at all. But her love had grown strong, and she wanted nothing more than to admit it to him...and hear him say the same in return.

One of the assistant producers stuffed her in a side room, and she paced. She had no idea when the taping was supposed to begin and whether she would be first. She didn't know if being first was good or bad since they could edit the show any way they liked. Her palms began to sweat and that reminded her of the lobster incident. She ran over to the mirror to check herself out. Her long, narrow face told her she wasn't having another allergic reaction. Plus, she could still breathe...mostly.

Renee inspected her hair, which she put back into a bun to keep out of her way. She even curled a few strands around her face to give herself a romantic style. Janice came over the day before with a new batch of dresses for her to examine. She chose a classy wine-colored dress with an empire waist. The velvet bodice was soft underneath Renee's fingers, and the satin skirt would reflect the studio lights and make the outfit look stunning.

Though Renee believed she looked better than she had during any other taping, her appearance didn't matter...it never had. This was about love...and Ben.

"Hey, Lockhart." Mike stuck his head inside the door. "We're ready for you on set."

"Already?" Renee asked. She was glad they weren't making her wait any longer, but she expected at least a slight delay. She followed Mike out the door, almost certain he had glee on his face. He was probably glad the show was almost over. It had been a smashing success all over town, but the local nature likely meant a lot of extra work for him. Renee tried to put herself in his shoes. She caused him even more trouble than the show. As they got closer to the back of the set, she reached a hand out and placed it on Mike's shoulder.

"Thanks, Mike," she said. "For everything. I wasn't the easiest person to work with, but I really appreciate all of the things you did to make this happen. Without you, I wouldn't have found Ben."

Mike's face fell a little. "Um, no problem," he said briskly. "You're going to go around this corner to the set. We'll start rolling as soon as you hit the lighted area, okay?"

Renee nodded and smoothed the dress down over her hips. She wished her outfit had pockets. She desperately needed something to do with her hands. Hopefully soon she would have a dandelion to hold. She took a deep breath and rounded the corner. She didn't want to put the moment off any longer.

As Renee stepped into the light of the studio stage, she raised her eyes and glanced around. The set was breathtaking. A stone path lined the center of the set with dandelions and other colored flowers lying around it. A small waterfall trickled water over rocks into a pond in a corner. As Renee began to walk, she searched the scene and noticed an archway at the end of the walkway.

Dandelions and twinkling white lights decorated the arch, but as soon as Renee laid eyes on Ben, nothing else mattered. She was on the right path to the man she loved, and she couldn't wait to reach him. She knew she rushed too fast when her toe caught one of the stones, and she stumbled. Steadying herself, she caught Ben's eyes and smiled. It was fitting that she stumble into his arms on the night of the finale. Tripping was all she'd been doing since the beginning. But as long as she ended up with him, she really didn't care how she got there.

Once Renee stood in front of Ben, tears welled up in her eyes. This was the moment she'd waited for all her life. To finally tell someone she loved them, and to hear the sentiment returned. She took a deep breath and tried to lose herself in Ben's expression.

Renee squinted up at Ben. Something was different. His eyes had a hard edge to them, and she was unsure as to how to translate his appearance. Perhaps he had already seen Tracy and was reeling from the breakup. She couldn't be sure, and she didn't like it. There was nothing she could do now but wait and hear what he had to say.

"Renee." Ben took her hands into his. "You have surprised me since the beginning of the show. I couldn't believe it when you caught fire."

Renee chuckled, trying to loosen the tight knot forming in her shoulders.

"No one else had the nerve to push me into the pool. And when your dress ripped, you handled it with such…flair."

Renee wondered if he would list everything she'd done wrong during the taping sessions.

"I am proud to say I witnessed you standing up to that monkey, and no girl can wreck a car like you."

Renee's her heart swelled. The details of their romance were unique and included one screw up after another on her part, but it brought them together and she loved every minute of it. Ben was taking his time for the cameras, but having their special moment on film would be priceless in the future.

"You continued to surprise me, Renee," Ben said softly. "Up until the very end. What surprised me the most, however, was learning why you auditioned in the first place."

The room began to spin as Renee felt the blood drain from her face. What was he talking about?

"It is because of those motives that I have to let you go."

"Wait, what?" Renee blurted as his hands slipped out of hers.

"I'm sorry, Renee." Ben's expression hardened. "I know you used me. I have enjoyed spending time with you, and I wish you all the best in your career."

Renee blinked. He knew. Somehow, Ben heard her reasons for trying out for the show, and why she stuck around even when she wasn't enraptured with him at first. But he didn't know she had fallen for him in the process. She couldn't believe he was blind to her love.

"But wait, Ben," Renee stuttered. "You don't understand. You have to let me explain."

"Explain all you want, Renee, nothing will change." Ben spoke through his teeth. "There's another woman involved here."

Renee cheeks flamed. "Are you saying you're in love with Tracy?"

"I'm choosing Tracy," Ben said with force. "You've had your moment in the spotlight. I hope you get the new job."

Renee wanted to grab the necktie from his tuxedo and wipe the tears from her face. At least she would have one last part of him to take away with her.

"But Tracy..." Renee wanted to tell him she wasn't right for him.

"It's for the best." Ben put his hand on Renee's back and turned her toward the path. "Goodbye, Renee."

Renee began walking without realizing her feet were moving beneath her. She went through the motions while understanding the city was watching. She had to leave with as much grace as possible. At that point, what else could she do? With no idea how Ben found out her secret, and no clue as to why he took it so hard, she had few options. But she was certain about one thing...her heart was utterly and completely broken.

As she arrived at the side of the set, hands propelled her away from the lights and the heavenly flowers. Someone pressed her down into a chair and put a water bottle in her lap. She drank a little, though not nearly enough to replace the stream of tears coursing down her cheeks.

"Time for your interview," a camera guy said as Renee stared in disbelief.

Renee looked straight ahead, trying to think of something to say. In the background, Tracy squealed in delight. Ben probably asked her to accept the final dandelion. He wanted to be with her.

"No comment." Renee pushed the lens away as she stood and raced from the studio. She needed to get out of there as fast as possible. She wanted to put as much space between her and the romantic set as she could…especially knowing Ben had Tracy in his arms. The show was over. She and Ben were over. Her hope for love was over.

# CHAPTER TWENTY-SEVEN

RENEE IGNORED ALL phone calls to her apartment over the next few days. Her friends and co-workers kept calling to check up on her, but no one knew how the show ended, and she couldn't face anyone without showing her heartbreak. Once the last episode aired, going out in public would be even worse, but at least she wouldn't have to explain what went wrong. Everyone would already know.

When Janice arrived at her door and almost beat it down just before the final show aired, Renee gave up resisting. Having a shoulder to cry on might be nice. And she had to face the real world eventually.

"Girl, where have you been?" Janice asked as Renee opened the door. "And why haven't you showered?"

Renee pulled at her t-shirt, which she wore over hole-ridden sweat pants. She had her hair back in a greasy ponytail. She looked her worst.

"Does this mean no happily ever after?" Janice placed the take-out meal on the living room coffee table. "I understand you're not supposed to tell anyone, but come on, the show's about to air."

Renee heard the concern in Janice's voice. She wasn't trying to get the drop on the show. She simply wanted to comfort Renee.

"Oh, Janice." Tears formed in Renee's eyes yet again.

"Come here, baby." Janice held her arms out to Renee, and she collapsed into them. "It's okay." Janice stroked her hair. "That man didn't recognize a good thing when he had it right in front of him."

Renee sobbed for a few minutes and then plopped down onto the couch, emotionally exhausted.

"What happened?" Janice asked softly.

"I really don't know." Renee blew her nose. "I mean, I was ready to tell him I loved him."

"Wait, love?"

Renee nodded. "Without a doubt. I wanted to be with him."

"But he didn't feel the same?"'

"That's just it. I think he did."

They turned to the TV as the commercials ended, and the theme song for the show sounded.

"Maybe this will give you some answers." Janice waved toward the screen. "In the meantime, you need to eat. You look like you haven't had a meal in days."

Janice was right, Renee hadn't. She accepted the open container of Chinese food with a grateful smile, but she knew she wouldn't be able to force down more than a bite or two.

Janice and Renee watched the show unfold, and Janice cackled when Renee slapped the misbehaving monkey. "I cannot believe you just did that," she said between loud laughs.

Renee chuckled as well. It came across even funnier than she expected. She had to hand it to herself...she was entertaining.

Janice quieted as Renee and Ben had dinner on screen and danced under the twinkling lights and the changing sky. As the picture faded to black and the loud commercials came on, she shook her head. "At this point, I can't see how he wouldn't pick you."

"Me either," Renee admitted. She was too close to the matter, but the way Ben looked at her...it seemed obvious his desire mirrored hers. She set down the take out container and leaned forward as Ben greeted Tracy for their date.

Ben and Tracy had a fancy dinner in some ballroom. Despite the surrounding romantic and elegant atmosphere, Ben kept his distance from Tracy. Halfway through the meal, Tracy leaned in. "There's something you need to know about Renee," she said.

Renee felt Janice's eyes on her as they watched in horror. Tracy laid out Renee's master plan...to heighten her public profile to get on the morning show at the radio station. She needed to make the city love her in order to be considered for the job. The way Tracy delivered the news, it was no wonder Ben hated her. He didn't have a choice but to pick Tracy in the end.

Had Janice not been there, Renee would have turned the TV off right then. She didn't want to see any more. She tried to tune it out because seeing Ben and Tracy dance and gaze at one another with stars in their eyes was too much. Watching them kiss was even worse.

"Look at me," Janice said when the tears took over Renee's cheeks again. "Look at me," she commanded.

Renee turned on the couch and obeyed. From the corner of her eye, she could still see Ben and Tracy making out.

"You love that man, do you not?"

Renee nodded. Her love existed, though she needed to examine it closer after seeing the way Ben acted with Tracy.

"You need to concentrate on what you had with him and believe in it. I don't care what he said or did. Believe in that love, you got me?"

Renee wiped the tears from her face with the back of her hand. A tiny sliver of hope rose in her heart. Janice was right. She gave up too easily. If Ben was the man she was meant to love for the rest of her life, she needed to give him a second chance...the opportunity to choose again.

She watched Ben turn her away on the screen and wasn't sure how to do it. Once she stumbled off the set, Janice snapped the TV off.

"We don't need to see anymore," she said. "What are you going to do about this?"

Renee thought it over, and a plan formed. It wasn't much, and it likely wouldn't bring Ben back to her, but it was the least she could do. She wanted to tell the city how she felt, and she needed to apologize to everyone involved. Then she could move on, though brokenhearted, with a clean conscious.

# CHAPTER TWENTY-EIGHT

RENEE STARED AT Chuck across the counter. "100.4 KGBR... Goooood morning." He smoothly addressed the city through the microphone. "We have a special segment planned today. With us this morning is our very own Renee Lockhart, runner-up on *Accept This Dandelion*. We'll get her thoughts on the show soon. We also have a big announcement you'll want to hear. That's all coming up next."

Chuck pressed a few buttons and turned off his microphone before swiveling his chair toward Renee. "That was some finale." He shook his head. "What a bummer."

Renee figured people would to act strangely around her for a while. No one knew what to say or do when they saw someone get their heart broken on TV.

"It's okay, Chuck." She wanted to believe it as much as she could. "I'm going to be fine."

"You are." He nodded. "You certainly are."

When the next song ended, Chuck pushed buttons like mad and got them back on the air with the theme music from the TV show playing behind their voices.

"Thank you to Renee Lockhart for being with us this morning. Renee, I don't want to ask you any questions. I'm going to turn things over to you and let you have your say. The airwaves are yours."

Renee gave Chuck a grateful smile. They discussed this before going on the air. She didn't need an interview. Their manager wouldn't be happy, but she would take the blame, not Chuck.

"Thanks, Chuck. Today, I want to tell the listening audience everything I didn't tell Ben. When I auditioned for the show, I had only one thing on my mind, and it wasn't love. I wanted everyone who saw the show to learn my name." Renee took a breath and continued. "I desperately wanted to replace Claudia right here on KGBR. Being on the morning show is a dream I've had for years."

Renee glanced at Chuck, who leaned back in his chair. "When I found out Ben McConnell was the bachelor on the local show, I almost ran the other way. His reputation intimidated me, and I didn't think there was any way I would be able to fall in love with someone like him."

*Here comes the hard part.* "But I went ahead with the show with my own selfish reasons in mind. I knew I wouldn't find love, but at least I had the chance to heighten my public profile, so, with any luck, I could get the job here at KGBR."

Renee took a deep breath. "The problem was everything I thought about Ben was wrong. And I *did* fall in love with him. That's right, I said it. I love Ben McConnell. Despite what he decided to do and who he may chose, I love him. Part of me always will. Even if our paths never cross again in this world."

Renee's hands shook. She was nearing the end of her time, and she couldn't believe what she was about to do. "And so, as an apology to Ben and to those who watched the show, I want to ask the managers here at KGBR to take my name out of the running for the morning show position. I would love nothing more than to be here with you, Chuck, but I don't deserve the job. I used Ben...the TV station...and the viewers. No one wants listen to a girl like that every morning."

Chuck's jaw dropped. He, of all people, understood how hard it was to get into the early time slot. For someone who loved being on the radio as much as Renee did, dropping out of the running was unthinkable.

"To wrap things up," Renee continued. "I want to address Ben if I could. Ben, I don't know if you're listening today, but if you're out there, I offer you my heartfelt apologies. I taped the show with my own ulterior motives, and I'm sorry. You didn't deserve to be used. But I can't and never will apologize for how I ended up feeling about you...the way I still feel. Ben McConnell, I love you. I truly believe you're the one I was meant to be with for the rest of my life. I am devastated you don't feel the same way, but I completely understand."

Renee turned to Chuck after ignoring him during her confession. It wasn't right to stare at him while admitting her love for Ben. "Thank you, Chuck, for letting me have this time. I appreciate the job you do here at KGBR, and I hope you find a great partner to fill Claudia's shoes."

Chuck's mouth hung open as the heavy studio door banged against the wall, and Janice stormed the room. She grabbed the microphone in front of Renee and swiveled it toward her.

"Now you listen here, Mr. McConnell. Renee told you quite a bit just now, but she didn't tell the full story. She didn't go to that audition solely with ulterior motives in mind. She went because I practically pushed her out the door. That's right, I signed her up for the show because she's one of the loveliest people I know, and I wanted her to meet someone. Blind dates don't seem to work, and she never lets me set her up with my cousin, but for some reason, I managed to talk her into the show. It was out of her comfort zone, but she did it. And now I know why. She did it for you. It was all for you. If you can't appreciate that, then you don't deserve her."

Chuck adjusted his microphone and leaned forward. Janice held her hand up to stop him from speaking. "Renee Lockhart is the kindest, sweetest woman I know. She went on your show because I made her...no other reason. She stayed because of you. Now that, Mr. McConnell, is all you need to know." Janice put her hand down, and a stunned Chuck finally found his voice.

"There you have it, folks, Janice Cloud having her say on the matter." Chuck started the commercial block and briskly turned the microphones off.

With nothing more to say, Renee pushed her rolling chair away from the counter, stood, hugged Janice tightly, and left the studio.

"DRIVE FASTER," BEN commanded.

"It's rush hour, sir, I'm going as fast as I can."

Ben shook his head in frustration as he beat his fist against the window. He needed to arrive now. He couldn't let her get away without having his say. It was only fair.

RENEE PLODDED BACK to her office and closed the door. She would have to answer plenty of questions from her manager later, but for now, she wanted to be alone. She had KGBR on in the background of her office, as usual, and she listened as Chuck continued the show.

"Well, Renee Lockhart took care of the announcement we were planning to make. After our interview with her, the good people here at KGBR were going to offer her the morning show position opposite yours truly. But now…since she turned it down before receiving the offer…I don't know who we'll hire."

Renee never heard Chuck flustered before, and she was relieved when he started a song. She'd done it. The position she always dreamed about could have been hers. But none of it meant anything without Ben. She hurt him in a way no one deserved and because of that, she needed to punish herself. She couldn't take the job knowing she climbed over him to secure it.

Renee turned on her computer, intending to write some scripts from the requests piled up on her desk. She had a lot of work to catch up on and burying herself in the daily grind would be the best way to move back into the real world. She would get over Ben. She had to.

After a few more sets of songs, Renee realized the first script she tried to write was still laying before her with only one word written. All she had was the company's name. She scooted her chair away from her computer and put her head in her hands. What was she going to do?

"We're back here on 100.4 KGBR, thanks for listening." Chuck's voice sounded through the small radio on her desk. "With us now is a special surprise guest. I can't even believe it. For the second time today, I am handing over the reins to the microphone. Thanks for coming in. The floor is all yours."

Renee expected her manager's voice to come next. He might be going on the air to explain Renee's monologue. Perhaps he had decided who would be on the morning show opposite Chuck instead of her. There were several candidates, and any one of them could fill the position instead.

"Uh, hello." A deep voice filled her office. Renee's head shot up, and her ears tuned in to the small speaker on her desk radio.

The man cleared his throat. "Sorry. I'm not used to this."

"Right," Chuck interceded, throwing his guest a line of help. "You're more accustomed to TV."

The guest laughed nervously. Renee knew that laugh. Ben.

"I wanted to answer Renee's comments." Renee stood and moved toward her door, stopping with her hand above the knob. "I feel bad for how we left things, and she needs to know I heard her say she was sorry, and I'm not holding a grudge. She probably shouldn't have kept the information from me, but she was true to herself and the viewers in every other way."

Renee smiled through her tears. Ben forgave her. She could move on knowing that he was over the hurt she caused him. But now, she had to get out of there. She didn't want to see him. Her heart was too newly broken. She turned the knob and pushed the door open. She glanced furtively up and down the hall. Clear. Renee rounded the corner, her eyes on the back exit door. She was almost to the end of the hallway when fingers surrounded her wrist and jerked her to a halt.

"Where do you think you're going?" Janice asked.

"I don't want to see him."

"You mean you wanted him to hear you out but you're not going to do the same?"

The look on Janice's face told the story. She was disappointed in Renee.

"I'm not asking you to go into the studio and face him. Just listen." Janice tugged Renee's hand and led her into the nearby empty engineer's office.

His desk radio was off, but with one click, Janice turned it on. She dialed the volume up and Renee leaned against the wall closest to the door. She could still make a quick escape if the need arose.

"Renee," Ben said as Renee stood frozen. "I want you to take the job here at KGBR. It's your dream, and if you turn the job down, I'll feel like I held you back."

Renee's shoulders sagged. Ben came all the way to the studio to let her know he heard on-air apology. That was huge. It meant even more that he stepped around his hurt and encouraged her to take the job. Any other man would have enjoyed letting her accept her punishment.

"More than anything, Renee, I needed to tell you something too. Because I wasn't honest with you either."

Renee frowned, her white knuckled fingers grasping the door handle.

"When I told you I didn't want to be with you, I lied. I was hurt, and I didn't know what to do, so I ran from you. But Renee, you need to know this…I love you too. You're the first person I've ever said that to in my life, and I wouldn't be surprised if you were the last." Ben hiccupped. "Thanks, Chuck, for letting me drop in on you like this." He hiccupped again. "Pardon me. I wanted the listeners to know I forgive Renee and love her with all my heart." Hiccup.

Chuck wrapped up the break and started another song, but his voice was merely background noise. She stared at the radio, wondering what she missed Ben say when she was in the hall between offices. Her guilt caused her to flee and hearing Ben's admission seemed to have paralyzed her.

Janice placed one hand on each of Renee's shoulder. Renee felt a subtle shake as she focused her eyes on her friend's face.

"What do I do?" She searched Janice's features.

"Honey, I think you know the answer to that. Go get that boy."

Renee's hands shook as Janice gave her a shove toward the office door. The studio was a direct shot from where she stood. She quivered when the door moved, and Chuck's loud voice echoed down the hall. Renee took a couple of steps. When Ben stepped out of the studio, she stopped dead in her tracks.

"Thanks again, Chuck." Ben waved and allowed the door to close. His chin sank to his chest.

Ben turned and caught her eye. "Hello, Renee." She heard hesitation in his voice, but smiled when he hiccupped again.

"What's with the hiccups?"

"I'm nervous."

"Radio makes you nervous?" Renee asked. "More nervous than TV?"

"It wasn't so much the airwaves that got to me." Ben took a few steps forward. His chest heaved again as he held in another convulsion. "It was more the things I said."

"You really accept my apology?" Renee cut the distance between them in half by taking several quick steps in his direction.

"I absolutely do. I can't blame you for your motives in the least."

"Why not?"

"I explained it on the air."

"I missed part of your broadcast." Renee didn't want to admit that she'd been trying to flee. She wondered if Janice hid in the office near the exit with her ear to the door, straining to hear the conversation taking place.

Ben put his hands in his pockets and casually moved a few more steps toward Renee. "After I told Chuck I forgave you, I said I couldn't blame you for using the show to gain popularity in the

[193]

city." Ben's shoulders jerked up with another hiccup. "I did the exact same thing."

"What? How?" Renee inched forward.

"I wanted to fall in love, but you've seen what the media says about me. No one thought I could really do it. I've been painted the playboy bachelor for years in this city. I thought the show would be a good way to change my reputation. Sure, it was a shot at finding someone special, but even if I didn't, I figured I could pick a winner and stick with her long enough to change the way people looked at me. At least I hoped."

Renee pursed her lips. "We were after the same things."

"Exactly. How can I fault you for using the show when I was doing it too?"

"You can't."

Hiccup. They were no more than three feet apart now.

"What about Tracy?" Renee asked. If Ben loved her and wanted to be with Renee, their union would cause Tracy hurt.

Ben shrugged. "We broke up about an hour after the show aired. Women's intuition...she knew I loved you. And she didn't want to be anywhere near a guy who was smitten with someone else."

Renee put her hand on his arm. "So, what does this mean?"

"I love you, Renee."

Renee waited for him to hiccup, but no sounds came from his throat. His steady gaze told her everything she needed to know.

"I don't care how many times you wreck cars, catch fire, do silly dances, and slap monkeys or anything else. I love you. In fact, those are a few of the reasons I fell in love with you in the first place." Ben removed his hand from his pocket and traced his fingers down her arm until he found her hand.

"I'm just a weed, Ben. Are you sure you can put up with me?"

"Renee." Ben took the final step and drew her into his arms. "Didn't you know dandelions are better than flowers? They spread their yellow joy farther and faster than any flower. Though some people take them to be a pest, the special ones recognize their beauty. The only thing is, I don't want you to turn to white puff and spread yourself around." Ben tightened his grip and placed his face close to hers. "I want you to stay right here with me."

Renee tilted her face up to look into his eyes. The hard expression she'd seen at the final taping was gone. What remained was pure love and acceptance. She was a weed, she was positive of that. She couldn't do anything right, but somehow, she had done everything she needed in order to get the man of her dreams.

"Ben," she whispered. "I love you too."

Ben closed the last inch between them and allowed his lips to meet hers.

Renee melted into his arms and allowed herself to float away into his kiss. Nothing had ever felt so completely right. She wanted the moment to continue forever so the tingle in her toes would never end.

"Who-hoo!" a shout rang from down the hall. "Who-hoo!"

Ben jerked his head back, and Renee whirled around. Janice ran past them, her arms raised as she shouted. "Who-hoo! It's official. Does everyone hear me?" Her voice got softer as she did a lap around the studio offices. "Who-hoo!"

Renee turned back to Ben. "Who-hoo is right. I never thought this could happen in a million years."

"You and me both. But I couldn't be happier that it did."

"Did you really hiccup live on the air on the KGBR morning show?" Renee asked.

"Did you really light yourself on fire on TV?" Ben replied.

Renee pressed her forehead against Ben's chest.

"Two can play at that game. And no offense, but I think I'd win every time," Ben challenged.

"Okay, okay." Renee held her hands up, but Ben didn't loosen his grasp on her waist. "You win. When it comes to faux pas, I am the master."

Ben smiled and grabbed one of Renee's hands to place it on his chest. "You're right. I do win."

Renee wanted to freeze the moment. She was lost in Ben's eyes, and her surroundings melted away. She was in love. And the man she loved returned her affections. Nothing in the world would ever be the same again. It would be better.

"Renee." A voice interrupted down the hall. "Get here bright and early Monday. Chuck and Renee in the morning goes live at five."

Renee broke the spell between Ben and her and stood on her tiptoes to see her manager waving a folder at her.

"Don't be late," he said.

Renee lowered herself and looked at Ben again. He nodded at her. "You deserve it."

"I don't deserve you."

Ben turned to her. "I'm just a weed, like you."

Renee threaded her arm through Ben's and began to lead him toward the exit. They had a life to start. Once they were outside, Ben released her hand and bent in the grassy area next to the exit. When he turned toward her, he had a bright yellow dandelion in his hand.

"Will you accept this dandelion?" he asked.

Renee took in the sad little yellow weed. It sure had caused her a lot of trouble. But as she focused her gaze past it and onto the man that stood behind it, she knew he was worth every ounce of humiliation, worry, and everything else she had gone through with the show.

"My last dandelion?" Ben stood, waiting for her reply.

"Without a doubt." Renee plucked the dandelion from his hand and put it behind her ear. It would wilt and shrivel in a matter of seconds, but Ben had seen her in worse ways. The dandelion meant a lot to her, but she didn't want anything between her and Ben...not even a pesky weed.

Renee threw herself into Ben's waiting arms and lost herself in his kiss. She'd always found dandelions beautiful, but she would never look at one quite the same way again.

## ABOUT THE AUTHOR

Brooke Williams is a sleep deprived stay at home mom/freelance writer/author. She attributes her humor to her two young children for keeping her in the lack of sleep realm on a permanent basis. Brooke is a former radio announcer and producer who also did a brief stint as a TV traffic reporter. She has been married to her husband since 2002, but since he seldom laughs at her jokes, she had to start writing to get them out. Brooke writes novels as well as articles and other items for clients on a freelance basis during the one hour a day her daughters allow her the time. Check some of her other novels, which include "Someone Always Loved You," and "Wrong Place Right Time."

Thank you for your Prism Book Group purchase! Visit our website to enjoy free reads, great deals, and entertaining, wholesome fiction!

http://www.prismbookgroup.com